LIFETIME GUARANTEE

CATHY GILLEN THACKER

Harlequin Books

TORONTO • NEW YORK • LONDON
AMSTERDAM • PARIS • SYDNEY • HAMBURG
STOCKHOLM • ATHENS • TOKYO • MILAN

For Sarah,
our sweet and charming
adventurer and animal lover,
who from the very first
has always wanted to be
at the center of the action,
and whose greatest pleasure
comes from helping others

Published November 1989

First printing September 1989

ISBN 0-373-16318-5

Copyright © 1989 by Cathy Gillen Thacker. All rights reserved. Except for use in any review, the reproduction or utilization of this work in whole or in part in any form by any electronic, mechanical or other means, now known or hereafter invented, including xerography, photocopying and recording, or in any information storage or retrieval system, is forbidden without the permission of the publisher, Harlequin Enterprises Limited, 225 Duncan Mill Road, Don Mills, Ontario, Canada M3B 3K9.

All the characters in this book have no existence outside the imagination of the author and have no relation whatsoever to anyone bearing the same name or names. They are not even distantly inspired by any individual known or unknown to the author, and all incidents are pure invention.

® are Trademarks registered in the United States Patent and Trademark Office and in other countries.

Printed in U.S.A.

"About the other night."

They stepped into the cooling autumn air as Ross began to talk.

Linda had been hoping he wouldn't bring up their impulsive kiss. She had been flirting with him a bit too much, and she blamed her mood on the flirtatious dress she'd worn to the fund-raiser, and the suave, handsome way he'd looked in his tux. "We're both adults, Ross. We can handle a simple kiss."

His fingertips slid under her chin, and he raised her face to his. "Is that all it was?" he asked softly. "It felt like more to me."

And to me, she thought wistfully. "No, Ross," she lied. "It wasn't. Dating would complicate our partnership. Can't we remain friends?"

He looked doubtful, but then he caved in. She tried to ignore the warm glint in his eyes, eyes that harbored something more. "Okay. We can be friends," he said. Then he added mysteriously, "For now."

ABOUT THE AUTHOR

Cathy Gillen Thacker has always enjoyed penning family-oriented stories. She comes from a large family herself, and now lives with her husband and children in Texas. Originally from Ohio, she attended Miami University, taught piano for a number of years, then turned to writing. She looks forward to capturing her adolescent children on paper as they mature.

Books by Cathy Gillen Thacker

HARLEQUIN AMERICAN ROMANCE
143–A FAMILY TO CHERISH
156–HEAVEN SHARED
166–THE DEVLIN DARE
187–ROGUE'S BARGAIN
233–GUARDIAN ANGEL
247–FAMILY AFFAIR
262–NATURAL TOUCH
277–PERFECT MATCH
307–ONE MAN'S FOLLY

HARLEQUIN TEMPTATION
47–EMBRACE ME, LOVE
82–A PRIVATE PASSION

HARLEQUIN INTRIGUE
94–FATAL AMUSEMENT
104–DREAM SPINNERS

Don't miss any of our special offers. Write to us at the following address for information on our newest releases.

Harlequin Reader Service
901 Fuhrmann Blvd., P.O. Box 1397, Buffalo, NY 14240
Canadian address: P.O. Box 603,
Fort Erie, Ont. L2A 5X3

Preface

Having grown up in a large midwestern family, I've come to notice how birth order influences your character, life choices, profession. It has always been a personal fascination of mine, but one that's also winning new converts interested in family dynamics. In fact, the study of birth order is becoming an important new field, helping to provide keys that will unlock the understanding of ourselves and ultimately improve relationships.

LIFETIME GUARANTEE is the second in a three-book spinoff series dealing with birth order, and how it has affected the adult children of the Harrigan clan, a prominent Texas family, all in their 30's, who've reached crucial stages in their lives. This book focuses on the youngest child, Linda Harrigan: a spirited teacher and educational pioneer, and her burgeoning relationship with banker Ross Hollister—a man who, in the end, can make or break her dreams.

What is a youngest child? Well, the consensus seems to be that the baby of the family is a real "people person." An outgoing charmer, the youngest is affectionate, and likes to entertain others, often by being the family clown. Typically, she is spoiled and coddled and overprotected one minute and then ignored the next.

The baby of the family is used to being "put down" by her other siblings, and hence usually develops a determined, single-minded attitude about whatever she tries to accomplish. Still, she often feels underrated, as her accomplishments win less applause from her parents than her older brothers and sisters received—not because they are any less spectacular, but because the parents have seen and experienced it all before.

The youngest has an added advantage: she gets a lot of instruction from older brothers and sisters. This lack of constant parental attention also allows the baby of the family to get away with a lot, so she does what she wants or feels is necessary and worries about repercussions later.

And last but not least, the youngest child is left to fend for herself, the downside being that she can sometimes be almost too independent. But this same sink-or-swim treatment makes her strong and gregarious. She's capable and able to stand on her own.

Chapter One

"What is that funny music, Daddy?" four-year-old Kimberly asked suspiciously the moment they arrived, her blond brows knitted together in perplexity. Bangs the color of cornsilk fell across her forehead, and long silky strands fell over her small shoulders and down her back. Nervously she plucked at the hem of her smocked pink dress, and crossed and uncrossed her black patent leather shoes, putting one toe over another.

"Hmm. I don't know." Ross parked his Mercedes station wagon next to the curb, his own curiosity and the breezy splendor of the autumn day prompting him to leave the car windows down. "It sounds like mariachi music." The notes were floating out through the open windows of the elegant ranch-style home in front of him. He checked the address of the Harrigan Enrichment Center on the notepad beside him—yes, this was the right place, all right. Why they'd play Mexican festival music in an Austin day-care home however, was beyond him. "Farmer in the Dell" would be more appropriate.

Kimberly hugged her battered brown teddy bear to her chest, and closed her eyes in a mixture of dread and anticipation. Ross waited, watching as she took a deep breath and sighed. At last she opened her eyes.

Ross gave her yet another moment to prepare herself. "Ready?" he asked gently, not wanting to rush her. She'd had enough adjustments to make the past few weeks. And the fact he was working night and day trying to get settled in his new job wasn't helping.

"Sure." Kimberly nodded seriously. She unbuckled her seat belt, her cherubic mouth set in a look of determination. "Let's go in now." Her ear still cocked toward the merry music, she slid forward until her feet hit the carpeted floor. The fingers of one hand curled around the door handle, while the other hand grabbed the door molding.

"Wait for me to come around and open your door, sweetheart," Ross said anxiously. "I don't want your fingers getting pinched."

"Okay, Daddy." Kimberly carefully withdrew her hand and waited patiently.

He noticed she still had her stuffed animal hooked in her hand when she climbed out of the car. "Maybe you should leave Bear here," he suggested gently. "We wouldn't want to lose him." Heaven help them if they lost her most cherished possession. She'd never sleep!

"Okay." Kimberly placed the teddy bear gingerly on the seat. Ross closed the door. Together they started up the walk.

The doorbell was answered on the first ring by a young woman in her early thirties. Visible in the large open room behind her were twelve dancing children, dancing with irrepressible liveliness, and another teacher, looking to be about twenty-one or -two. All were dressed in sombreros and brightly colored serapes. Kimberly stared at the activity, entranced.

"Greetings!" the young woman with the mane of dark curly hair and midnight blue eyes said. She cheerfully extended her hand. "I'm Linda Harrigan, director of the Center. How may I be of help to you?"

Ross slowly dropped his hand to his side. His first thought was that this woman was too pretty, too charming and spirited to be director of a preschool. His second thought was that she was exactly the type of teacher all preschoolers needed—confident, someone who would show them how to squeeze every ounce of joy out of life. And the other teacher there, still dancing in the background, looked equally competent and cheerful, if a bit young.

"I'm Ross Hollister. I called earlier in the week to get information on your program. You said I could drop by any time during school hours and take a look around."

"Right, I remember you. You had a lot of questions—very good questions, I might add," Linda said, returning his glance with easy candor. She had an openness about her, an obvious propensity for making others feel comfortable.

In his search for a school for Kimberly he had been braced for the friendly greeting that inevitably followed his arrival, which preceded the routine sales pitch each director gave about their particular establishment. But nowhere else had he seen such genuine friendliness. He found himself relaxing a bit, as he simultaneously hoped the rest of what he saw here matched his initial impression. He really wanted to find a place for Kimberly. She needed to learn how to play and get along with other children.

Linda Harrigan looked down at Kimberly and her voice brimmed with kindness. "And hello to you, too! What's your name?"

Kimberly moved closer to Ross, her shyness preventing her from responding. Ross felt a moment's pang that Kimberly had such a hard time dealing with other people, then reassured himself her shyness was something she would, with the help of the right school, outgrow.

The music continued in the large room. The children and teacher continued to dance, with varying degrees of efficiency and much enthusiasm. He had to speak loudly to be heard above the lively music. "Her name's Kimberly."

Linda smiled at his daughter. "Hello, Kimberly," she said softly, with a wave of greeting, her manner incredibly gentle.

Again Ross found himself drawn to the pretty director. He thought, but couldn't be sure, that she looked slightly disturbed by his daughter's timidity; and then considering, as if she were already thinking of ways to draw Kimberly out.

Linda looked back at Ross. A smile curved her generous mouth. "I'm glad you decided to come and visit the Center. Won't you come in?"

She stopped to introduce them to Glenna Schultze, the young teacher. "Glenna's been with me since she graduated from the University of Texas in August. She also has a degree in early-childhood education," Linda said.

Ross found the young woman to be as warm as Linda. She seemed to look for direction from Linda, which Linda provided, glancing at her watch. "I think it's time for afternoon recess," she said.

Glenna nodded cheerfully. "You read my mind!"

The two of them worked like a well-orchestrated team, with Linda turning the music down to a low murmur while Glenna informed their charges, "Okay, gang, enough social studies for today! Let's clean up and put everything back in our cubbies and then we can go outside for some fresh air and sunshine. Okay?"

"Okay," they all shouted back. While Linda looked on approvingly, the children scattered to do as Glenna bid, scampering over the carpeted floor of what had once been a huge family room. Ross took careful note of the surroundings.

He had to admit this private-home turned day-care center was geared for children. Kid-sized tables and chairs lined one wall, cubicles with toys another. In the middle was plenty of space for the children to play. The white-paneled walls were adorned with brightly colored cardboard cutouts of *Sesame Street* characters. The letters of the alphabet and numbers one through ten bordered the ceiling colorfully. In a sunny room off to the left, he saw two computers on small tables, a portable television and video recorder, an array of books, building blocks, puzzles, and several shelves of art supplies. The atmosphere was clean, relaxed and reassuring. Ross's estimation of the woman running the operation increased.

He watched as she removed her serape and sombrero and unself-consciously shook out her thick dark hair. Again he was struck by the amount of energy, enthusiasm and competence she exuded. There was a serenity about the place and Linda Harrigan, too. He could see the children all felt very secure. Even Kimberly began to relax as Linda showed them both around.

"Do you teach a lot yourself?" Ross asked.

"As often as I can," Linda answered, returning his smile easily. "I really like interacting with the children. I have to handle administration and funding, but I need to keep in touch with what's going on with each child, too."

"You feel that the individual is important?" Ross probed.

"Absolutely. All the children have to be happy before you can have a happy group. One unhappy child causes disruption within the entire group."

"So you encourage them to conform?"

"No, never. I encourage creativity and independent thinking. Of course they also get lessons in manners and deportment. And we offer practical instruction on how to answer the telephone or dial 911, what to do in the event of a fire, how to make cookies or green eggs and ham. We cover the gamut."

Ross had to admit the curriculum sounded fascinating, as well as first-rate. Kimberly, also, looked absorbed in everything Linda was saying. Her positive response to a strange place was comforting to see. "Do you have just the one class?" Ross asked, studying the computer equipment in the second classroom. He noted several shelves of software geared to children, everything from *Kids on Keys* and *Memory*

Master to *Math Rabbit* and *My Letters, Numbers, Words*.

Linda nodded, meeting his gaze sedately. For a brief moment, something akin to regret showed in her eyes. "For now," she admitted matter-of-factly. "We're currently trying to expand, but it's a very complicated process, to say the least."

"And the children actually use the computers? They're not too hard for them?"

"You'd be surprised at what they can do. And all our software is geared for ages three to six, so yes, they can work independently, without much help from either Glenna or myself." Linda glanced down, noting Kimberly was getting restless.

"Why don't we talk out back while the children play?" she suggested, her steady dark blue eyes on his, making him once again aware of her natural healthy beauty. She wore little makeup, but then she didn't need much, with her flawless complexion and sun-kissed cheeks. She was tall and slim, the top of her head coming just above his shoulder. She moved with an easy, captivating grace.

He wasn't sure what it was, but there was something about her that he found, well, compelling. So much so that he couldn't seem to stop watching her. Surprising, because no woman had affected him that way in a long time. God knew his first priority was to get through day by day, make his daughter happy. To see Kimberly was safe and well cared for. The life of a single parent might be trying, he thought ruefully, but it could still be very satisfying. Nonetheless, it was interesting to note that he wasn't immune to a woman's charm.

Oblivious to Ross's thoughts, Linda escorted them both outside, into the large, shady backyard with the wooden privacy fence. She smiled at his daughter, and said gently, "Kimberly, you're welcome to swing or play in the sandbox or climb on the slide, okay?" She looked at Ross again. "I'm sure you have a lot you still want to ask me."

Yes, he did. He was a stickler for thoroughness.

After some encouragement on his part, Kimberly eventually wandered off to explore the yard.

"She's very shy, isn't she?" Linda said, her expression turning thoughtful once again.

Ross nodded, repressing his own disappointment at his daughter's shyness. "Very, I'm afraid."

"Has she ever been in preschool before?"

"No." Ross had never really considered it necessary, but lately he had begun to reconsider, knowing it would be good for Kimberly to get over her bashfulness to be able to do well in kindergarten the following year.

Over by the slide two small jean-clad boys whooped it up, pretending to be superheroes, out to save the world.

Ross grinned, remembering a few such adventures himself. "That's Tad," Linda said, pointing to a rambunctious but fastidiously groomed boy with a thatch of black hair in a Prince Valiant cut. "And that's Dexter." She pointed to another equally boisterous little boy. His clothing and white blond hair were askew, and the remains of his lunch were smeared across the front of his shirt.

Impressed with the center and the kids, Ross commented softly, "You have quite an operation here. The best I've seen."

Linda smiled at the compliment and touched his arm lightly. "Look over there," she said.

Ross did and what he saw amazed him. Kimberly had stopped being a spectator and had joined in the line at the slide, participating in a way she had not done at the other centers they'd visited. When it came her turn, she climbed the steps with determination, only glancing at him once for support, before shoving herself down the slide. She landed on the soft sandy pit at the bottom with a thud, grinning broadly.

"This is something new?" Linda guessed, sharing in his excitement over his daughter's easy acclimation to the center.

That was an understatement. "What it is, is downright amazing," he said. "I've never seen her do this anywhere else—just go and join in."

"I'm glad she likes it here," Linda murmured, looking briefly as troubled as she was pleased by his revelation. Recovering, she said, "Let's see, what haven't I covered? Oh, yes, the curriculum. We've worked hard to create an emotionally nurturing and intellectually stimulating environment. We want the children to do more than memorize the alphabet and learn their numbers. We want them to imagine and invent and create. So we have special problem-solving activities every day for developing their higher-level-thinking skills."

Ross thought of the way the kids had been dancing when he'd arrived. "You teach social studies, too, I suppose?"

Linda nodded. "We want them to know more than just their own world. That's why we study other cultures—the food, the music, the language. And I believe I already mentioned that we also work on social skills. For instance, last week we did a unit on answering the phone." She grinned, remembering. "They had a riot because I incorporated that with a problem-solving lesson—what to do if you order pizza and it never arrives—and then videotaped the whole lesson à la *Candid Camera*. We played it back the next day."

"Do you have a set routine you follow every day?" He glanced over and saw that Kimberly was now on the swings.

Observing Tad and Dexter engaged in a mock battle that was getting a little too rowdy, Linda waved at them and shook her head. They frowned, but desisted. She turned back to Ross. "Snacks, lunches, and rest period are at the same time every day. Other than that, no, we don't follow a set routine or do math every day at nine-twenty. We prefer to mix things up, to surprise the kids. It keeps us all on our toes...." Across the yard, Glenna was telling the children that playtime would end in another five minutes. This was greeted with moans and groans from the troops, but no one seemed really to mind.

Except Ross. He was all too aware his time with Linda was coming to a close. He also knew he had finally found the school for his daughter.

"About Kimberly," he began, "how do I go about enrolling her here?"

In response Linda looked wistfully over at his blond daughter, then reluctantly up at him. Her eyes were awash with regret. "I wish I could take in more children, Mr. Hollister, but I can only care for twelve children at a time in my home, and I've got that many now. I do have a waiting list, though. You're welcome to join it."

Ross swallowed his disappointment. He had prayed for this kind of place for Kimberly, and so far in his exhaustive search he hadn't found anything remotely like it. In fact, none of the quality preschools had openings. "Do you foresee any vacancies soon? You see, I'm a single parent and my housekeeper just can't give Kimberly the stimulation she needs." He knew it was wishful thinking as soon as he spoke.

She shook her head regretfully, her eyes kind. It was obvious she hated to turn him down. "No. And even if I did, there are ten people in line before you. I'm sorry," she said. "I've been trying to expand, but it isn't easy. To lease a place in a commercial area, and employ additional staff, I'd need a lot of financing."

Ross frowned, wondering if she had looked in the right places. Business problems were something he could handle. "Have you been to the banks?"

"Yes, but to no avail." She sighed, remembering she wasn't anxious to go through the nerve-racking approval process again.

But Ross knew if a bank could see what he had, they'd know Linda and her business had great potential. And if that happened, Kimberly might have the perfect place to go to school. "Maybe you just haven't tried the right one. Look, I'm a banker." Acting on impulse, he handed her a card that said Ross Hollister, Branch Manager, with the name of his bank embossed in large colonial-styled letters. "I can't promise anything, but I'd like to try."

Linda studied the name on the card, then looked back at him.

"Drop by the bank and I'll see what I can do," he said.

Kimberly ran back to Ross's side, more animated and cheerful than she'd been in weeks. She knew by the look on his face he was ready to go. "Daddy, can we stay five minutes more?" she gasped breathlessly.

Linda smiled, then said, "Feel free to roam around as long as you like. It'll give you and Kimberly a better sense of the place."

"All right," Ross said. "Five minutes. But then we really have to leave."

LINDA WENT ROUND AND ROUND before she finally decided to do as Ross Hollister suggested and apply for a business loan at his bank downtown. Part of her indecision was due to past experience. It was no fun to apply for a loan and be turned down. And part of it was due to Ross Hollister himself. He was simply too attractive in that easy-going, innately masculine, all-American way she found personally lethal. With short, impeccably layered hair the color of cornsilk and vivid green eyes, he was too attractive for her comfort. Moreover he had an openness about him that was pleasant and enticing. When she stood next to him she felt pleasurably dwarfed by his rangy, broad-shouldered, athletic build. She liked the way he carried himself, his posture radiating a calm assurance. She liked his evenly balanced features and straight, no-nonsense nose and chin. Even his thick wheat-colored brows, with their intriguing center arch, fascinated her. Although she'd fought the attraction successfully during their first meeting, she sensed it would be all too easy to become distracted in subsequent interactions. She only hoped she didn't make a fool of herself at his bank.

Fortunately her application was handled by one of the loan officers, an efficient-looking older man. Ross Hollister did drop by very briefly at the end of the interview and tell her he'd personally review the application and put in a good word for her with the board of directors.

Feeling she'd conducted herself professionally, presented her case for receiving a loan well, she went home full of hope. But as several days passed with no word, her spirits sagged. And when Ross Hollister arrived unexpectedly at her home, right after closing on Thursday afternoon, she knew by the look on his face she'd been rejected again. "They turned me down, didn't they?" she said.

He nodded, his own unhappiness with the decision evident. "I'm sorry. But there are certain criteria that aren't met. The bottom line is you just don't have enough collateral—"

"Or the work history and experience as a day-care provider." Linda had heard the same excuse before, and she sighed.

"Maybe in a year or two..." he amended gently, looking for a moment as if he wanted to reach out and comfort her.

"I don't know why I'm so disappointed. That's what everyone else said, too," Linda said deceptively lightly.

"You could try small-business administration," he offered helpfully, edging nearer. Dressed in a charcoal linen suit, starched white cotton shirt and black silk tie, he looked both dashing and sympathetic.

Linda concentrated briefly on his tie, before returning her gaze to his face. The man exuded power, but even he was no miracle worker. "I already did." Her voice lowered another notch, as she maintained her easy, accepting tone. "I was turned down there for the same reasons. They said come back in a year or two, maybe they could help me then." Which unfortunately would be too late for Ross's daughter. A shame, Linda thought, because he would have been a nice man to get to know. So personable, obviously devoted to his daughter. Linda had always thought you could tell a lot about a man by watching how he interacted with children; if the tenderness he demonstrated with Kimberly was any indication, Ross Hollister was a class act all the way.

She bent and picked up a few scattered toys, replacing them on the shelves. He watched in silence for a minute, then said softly, "I wish I could do more."

"Look, forget it," she said, adopting a bright, cheerful tone. "You tried and thank you." Her motto had always been to hope for the best and to prepare for the worst; this instance was no exception.

He continued to watch her, his look pensive. As if he knew it was past time for him to move on, but didn't want to. "Well, good luck," he said finally.

Linda nodded. "Same to you." She offered him a wry smile, and then watched him go, unable to help sighing a little as she shut the door behind him. She knew she'd recover from her disappointment over the loan refused her; but harder to accept was the knowledge that, with the reasons for Ross Hollister and her becoming acquainted now eradicated, she knew it was unlikely their paths would ever cross again.

"SO, HOW'S THE SEARCH for a day-care center coming?" Ross's coworker, Francine Durbin, asked the following Thursday afternoon.

"It's not," he sighed, the depth of his frustration reverberating in his voice. "Kimberly and I have visited every center in north and central Austin. We found four that were, well, okay, I guess. One even had an opening."

"But?" Francine poured herself some coffee and sat down across from him. Happily married and the mother of three, she understood full well what he was going through.

"Kimberly just wasn't excited about any of them. And after Linda Harrigan's operation, they all looked dull. Kimberly's been asking about it."

"I know. The word on Linda Harrigan is that she's a terrific teacher, and a wonderful human being. I mean, everybody likes her."

"She's full of charm, all right," Ross said, frowning.

His frown wasn't because of his failure to get Kimberly into Linda Harrigan's preschool. The fact was he felt damned guilty for what had happened to Kimberly the past few years. He'd been so distracted by his grief over the unexpected death of his wife, he had stayed mostly to himself, and hence, in the process, allowed Kimberly to get excessively shy. Oh, she was comfortable around family and his housekeeper, but there her ease with people ended. In new situations, around strangers, she appeared withdrawn. And their recent move, the culture shock of leaving the more formal East for the laid-back Southwest, wasn't helping any.

But that wasn't all that was bothering him. He was still troubled because he knew deep down that he shared at least some responsibility for the accident that had taken Kimberly's mother's life. If only he had prevented Karen from driving that night, he thought. If only he'd listened to his gut instinct and made her stay home from her night class at the university. But he hadn't, and as a result of some bad weather, terrible luck, and his laissez-faire attitude, Karen had died.

Even now, two years later, he wasn't sure how much Kimberly was able to comprehend about her mother's death. But lately, as she watched more television and learned more about the world around her, she had begun to ask questions, to want to see pictures of her mother, to get explanations of why she had no mommy.

Feeling like he'd had a frog in his throat and a fist in his gut, he had explained as best he could about heaven. Kimberly had finally seemed to accept the notion that her mother was happy, watching lovingly over them from some distant, wonderful place.

But Kimberly was still missing a lot out of life, he knew, by not having a mother. And he was determined to make that up to her in whatever way he could. He might not be able to bring Karen back for Kimberly, he thought, but he could sure as hell make her life richer, and more meaningful, by getting her into a school where she would thrive.

"So what are you going to do?" Francine asked eventually, crossing her legs and sitting back in her chair.

Aware he had drifted off somewhat rudely, Ross shrugged and finished the last of his coffee. It was cold and bitter, and he grimaced as it went down. "I don't know. Kimberly still wants to go to Linda's school." In fact, she had her heart set on it.

Francine made a rueful sound and took another sip of her coffee. "Too bad American Heritage couldn't give her a loan. That would've worked out perfectly for you."

Yes, it would've, Ross thought.

Not that he didn't understand the loan committee's decision. They had valid reasons for withholding approval. Financially, Linda Harrigan couldn't swing an expansion alone, no matter how gifted a teacher she was.

If only she had a partner. Someone to cosign or put up collateral. Someone with a solid business background, a stable track record. Someone who, like himself, had some insurance money just sitting around in certificates of deposit. But it couldn't be just anyone she hooked up with, he knew. If that was the case he could probably fix her up with some outside investor right now, if she agreed. But even as he thought of it, he nixed the idea. No, to make a partnership work, Linda would have to find someone as committed to excellence as she was.

The next idea hit him with the swiftness of a lightning bolt, and Ross sat up straight in his chair. Of course, that was it. He'd just found the solution to both their problems!

WHEN LINDA OPENED her door a few hours later, she looked surprised to see Ross Hollister standing there before her. Caught off guard by his arrival, she paused in the portal. "Mr. Hollister, I—"

"I hope you don't mind my dropping by without calling first, but I had something to discuss with you," he said as she ushered him inside and shut the door behind them. "Something that can't wait."

"Oh?" She lifted a brow, looking perplexed but not unhappy to see him.

"You see, it came to me this afternoon. There is one other solution to your problem. Something we didn't discuss."

Her curiosity piqued, she opened the double doors to her living room and led him in. She sat and gestured for him to take the other sofa, facing her. She was dressed in vivid teal-blue sweats and bright red sneakers. Her mop of long dark curls was twisted and caught up in a silver clasp, with wisps trailing down her neck and onto her cheek. As she gazed at him attentively, her cheeks filled with color. "Go on. Please."

Ross didn't plan to disappoint her. In a businesslike tone, he said, "It occurred to me you could look for outside funding—from a private source. That way you wouldn't have to put up collateral."

Linda drew in a deep breath. "What are you saying? That I take in a partner?"

He nodded, his confidence growing. "I think it's the only solution," he said bluntly. "Although your credentials and reputation are excellent, you really don't have the business background necessary to expand your business successfully. Not without help."

Her smile vanished when he began to talk about her one shortcoming. She looked both miserable at the situation and perturbed with him for pointing out her weakness. "Then what's the point?" she asked irritably.

Ross could see she was wondering why he had come over. He leaned forward earnestly, determined to do this for Kimberly. He might not be able to give his child her mother back, but he could give her a safe, wonderful place during the days he couldn't be with her. His voice dropped a notch. "The point is, that all that could change if you would consider taking on a partner. Someone with the proper business credentials."

Linda's gaze narrowed and she remained silent.

She seemed to be deciding whether or not she could trust him. Ross decided to slow down and give her a moment to take it all in.

"I suppose you have someone in mind?" she asked tightly after a moment, still resenting his intrusion.

Now for the second shocker, he thought. He nodded and pointed to his chest. "I've got someone in mind all right. Me." She did a double take and he continued audaciously, not embarrassed to go on. "I'm always looking for a good investment. And I'll be frank—I really like what I've seen here."

Linda stared at him in stunned silence, then disappointment clouded her eyes. "Thank you, but no." When she sensed correctly he was about to protest, she continued firmly, "This is my business, and mine alone, and that's the way it's going to stay. Thank you for your offer, but the answer remains no."

He studied her bluntly, his mouth thinning unhappily. This turn of events he hadn't expected. "That's a rather shortsighted view," he retorted gruffly. He'd expected her to be more positive. Hell, why not admit it? Maybe even overjoyed at his generous offer.

"Perhaps, but it's the way I feel," she retorted in a voice that invited no further discussion.

He hesitated again, knowing he shouldn't push harder. And yet he couldn't resist working in one more plug. "If you change your mind..."

She shook her head firmly. "I won't." And on that note, she thanked him for stopping by, for considering her, then showed him out.

Moments later, Ross started his car and sat there, stunned by the abrupt, uncompromising way she had dismissed his idea. Glancing behind him to make sure the road was clear, he guided his Mercedes onto the shady, tree-lined street.

As he drove, he wondered at Linda's determination to go it alone, wondered at what she might've said but hadn't. Why the outright rejection? In fact, she seemed insulted by his proposed solution to both their problems. And now he was right back where he'd started, his stroke of genius cast aside as readily as yesterday's newspaper. Kimberly still had no place to go to school. She was still excessively shy—even dangerously. And he was fast running out of remedies to correct the situation.

"I'M SORRY. I don't see why you were so offended," Linda's oldest brother, Tom, said early Saturday morning. He'd come down to help her complete a project—make child-sized picnic tables for the back yard. "In fact, if you want the truth, I think you should be flattered this Ross Hollister was so impressed by what he saw that he wanted to buy into your business."

Linda sighed and rolled her eyes. Brothers! Why was it that, when you needed them most, they always took the opposite side? "It's important to me to do this on my own," she retorted stubbornly. She went to replace one tool and get another from the Peg-Board hanging on the garage wall.

"I know," Tom countered dryly, as he carefully sanded down the rough edges of the wood. "Regardless of the fact there are other people close to you—family, mind you—who would be more than willing to help out."

Linda measured a piece of wood and marked off where it needed to be cut. It infuriated her when other people presumed to know better than she did what was best for her. And when Ross Hollister had made his unexpected offer, she'd seen red. All she could think was that he felt she was incapable of handling her life, that she needed to be "rescued."

"I've been leaning on other people for too long, Tom." She also wanted Tom to support her, but maybe that was a foolish wish—he and Mike both were as bad as her parents had been when it came to protecting and pampering her. They'd started when she was an infant and hadn't stopped since—except for the years when she'd been married, when they had expected her husband, Gene, to take care of her. He had, and it'd almost smothered her.

Tom sighed, seeing her point. "I understand your need for independence, Linda, and your need to make your own choices without being subject to all sorts of unsolicited advice." He'd spent years tending bar at nights so he could devote himself to his first love—writing—during the day. "But I also know that time is slipping away from all of us. We're not as young as we used to be. I mean look at us. I'm thirty-nine. You're thirty-four. Mike's thirty-seven!"

She was all too aware of their respective ages; in fact it had been her turning thirty and realizing her life was almost half over that had precipitated her need to make a career change. She'd known she had to stop doing what other people thought was safe, and do what she wanted. She'd had to make something of herself, not just continue as a shadow and helpmate to her husband. Only Gene, her ex-husband, hadn't understood. Not that this was surprising. In the years they had been married, they had gradually grown in very different directions. She wanted more independence. Gene wanted a princess to direct and protect. She eventually felt trapped, and their split was painful but necessary, their divorce amicable.

Nonetheless, Linda was aware she had miles more to go in her struggle to attain her goals. And nothing was going to stop her.

"What's your point, Tom?" she asked wryly.

"I just don't want to see you wait too long to achieve your dream—especially when there is another way out for you," he said persuasively.

So he thought she should take in a partner, too. What Tom said made sense, Linda knew. Theoretically anyway, Ross was offering her the kind of help and support she needed to really get her school off the ground, to make it a reality instead of a dream. Thinking of all the children she could care for—children who were still on her waiting list—made her refusal bittersweet.

She looked at Tom, watching as his large hands lovingly smoothed the grain on the small table. Something else was wrong, she thought. Something else was on his mind. "This pensive mood of yours," she began slowly, "all this talk about time slipping away from us. What's up? Did you run into trouble on your book tour?" His first, it had been a cause for celebration and anxiety.

Tom shook his head. "No. Although there were a couple of autograph signings in the small bookstores when the fans were few and far between."

"Then what is it?"

He shrugged, frowning, and turned off the sander. "I don't know. The onset of a midlife crisis, maybe? My writing career is going great guns. I don't have to work two jobs anymore to support myself. I should be happy."

"But you're not."

"No." His expression turned even bleaker. "This is going to sound like a cliché, but more and more these days I feel like there's something missing in my life, something vital."

"A woman, maybe?" she teased reflexively, keeping her tone purposefully light. Inwardly, however, she was worried. It was unusual for Tom to be so down. He'd always been such a driven, goal-oriented person. It was disconcerting to see him so confused, set adrift.

At her teasing gibe, he grinned wryly and retorted in a deadpan tone, "No, Linda, I'm not missing a woman. In fact there have been plenty of those. Too many, maybe."

But none he'd wanted to stay, Linda thought.

"What then?" She sat cross-legged on the floor opposite him. It was funny, knowing her oldest brother needed her now in a way she usually needed him, but nice to be able to help out, too.

Tom shrugged as he struggled to put his inner turmoil into words. "I don't know. I guess what I regret is not having kids. A real home. A family of my own." He hesitated, then continued in a more emotional vein, "I look at Mike and I see what he's found with Diana. He's got a wife who loves him. He's got Kevin, and Carlos, and Ernie. His ranch for boys is growing—"

"Not to mention the fact that Diana's pregnant now," Linda said softly. "I know. I'm envious, too. Happy for them, but also aware that I want the same things for myself, and yet . . ."

"We're both so far from it," Tom added, then uttered a beleaguered sigh. In a sudden restless movement, he stood and stretched.

Linda got slowly to her feet. "There's another side of life—business, for instance," she countered.

He grimaced. "Ah, yes—business. And finishing up these tables is big business indeed."

She smiled as she watched him go back to work. Secretly she agreed with him. The other day when Ross Hollister had been there with his little girl, Kimberly, and she'd seen the love flow freely between father and daughter, she'd had a real sense of what she was missing.

LINDA WAS PUTTING the finishing touches on the lasagna for Monday's lunch when Ross called late Sunday afternoon. Without preamble, he got straight to the point, his low sexy voice doing unsettling things to her insides. "I hoped you might have reconsidered my offer by now. You never gave me a chance the other day to outline my idea."

The days that had passed had given her plenty of time to think. Linda knew she'd been abrupt with him, almost rude, and she'd been regretting the way she'd handled his proposal ever since. She kept thinking about all the children who would benefit if only she swallowed her pride and accepted Ross's offer. After all, what did it really matter how and why her school expanded, as long as it did? Tom was right. Maybe she was being foolish, by refusing to hear Ross out. What could it hurt to simply listen to what he had to say?

"How about having dinner with me this evening?" he asked genially.

Her ambition prodding her, Linda gave in. "All right. Name the time and place." Her going didn't necessarily mean anything, she told herself firmly.

"Dan McKlusky's, the Arboretum," he replied in a reassuring businesslike manner. "Say, six o'clock?"

Linda glanced at her watch. The restaurant was a nice one. No tie or jacket was required. In fact, Austin was such a laid-back city that she could get by just about anywhere in nothing dressier than slacks and a sweater. "All right, I'll meet you there." Her voice was as brisk and efficient as his had been.

"That's not necessary. I'll pick you up," he continued smoothly before she could object. "We may have to wait for a table and it'll be easier to find each other that way."

"All right," she said, disconcerted, feeling as if she was being very subtly railroaded into something she ought to at least want to resist, but strangely didn't. "I'll expect you around five forty-five?" In contrast to her inner turmoil, her voice was calm.

"See you then."

AS LINDA EXPECTED, Ross was punctual. What she was not prepared for was how sexy he looked in his navy sport coat and tailored slacks, the light blue shirt and tie. Aware he had dressed up slightly more than she, which proved, in her mind anyway, what a true Yankee he was, she greeted him formally. She also wondered if and when he ever loosened up. But there was no clue to that in the determined set of his jaw or the slightly remote look in his eyes.

Traffic was relatively light for a weekend evening, and they made it to the Arboretum in just under fifteen minutes. On the way they kept their conversation light and casual. He talked about his adjustment to the South while Linda wondered if a truly conservative businessman like Ross would ever really adapt to Austin's laid-back ambience. "So you like Austin then?" Linda inquired, as they were seated at a small, secluded corner table.

"Yes, although it's a change from Philadelphia," Ross said, looking around, apparently mystified by the casual dress of the patrons in the elegant restaurant.

Well, that was progress, Linda thought. He realized he was a tad overdressed. But then he'd probably known that at the outset, and decided to dress as he thought appropriate anyway. Would he have the same traditional approach in his business dealings?

Picking up the thin threads of the conversation, she probed casually, "You've never lived in the South?"

"Never lived anywhere outside of the Northeast, until now."

So he was a Yankee through and through. "You had no qualms about moving?" As she glanced at him expectantly, waiting for him to reply, she couldn't help but notice how closely he'd shaved. His thatch of cornsilk-colored hair was perfectly brushed, the strands falling precisely across his forehead, the tops of his ears, the nape of his neck. Linda's own hair was a tousled mass of silky dark curls she'd finger-combed into place and then forgotten.

He leaned back in his chair and said candidly, "Because of Kimberly, I had plenty of qualms about moving so far from home, but in the end the promotion to bank manager was too good to pass up." His forest green eyes narrowed reflectively. "So I took it."

Well, at least they had that much in common, Linda noted. They both took risks for their respective careers, though Ross's seemed particularly admirable.

The waitress returned with menus and glasses of iced tea. Although Linda knew the selection of entrées at her favorite restaurant by heart, she studied the menu to give Ross time to choose. When the waitress returned, they gave their orders, Linda going first while Ross surveyed her casually, noting without apparent emotion her gray silk blouse and roomy flannel trousers, the cranberry-red pullover, and red, high-heeled shoes.

"Austin's a very casual place," he said after the waitress departed. "Have you lived here long?"

"About sixteen years now. I grew up in Houston."

"Whereabouts?"

"The River Oaks section."

He was enough of a banker to know what that meant. His brows rose. "Wealthy parents?"

Linda nodded. "My father used to play professional baseball. When he retired he became a sportscaster for the Astros."

"And yet you ended up here."

"It's a wonderful place to settle." In fact, she had loved it while attending the Austin campus of the University of Texas. The city was warm and friendly, yet sophisticated enough to support a wonderful symphony orchestra and a wealth of progressive country music. Everywhere she went she found an eclectic mix of people—ranchers, engineers and scientists, Texas statesmen—all living in casual, perfect harmony.

He nodded, then said, "About my proposition the other day..."

Linda felt compelled to be honest with him. It was only fair he know how she still felt. "I agreed to hear you out as a courtesy, Ross. I'm still not looking for an active partner." She sensed that was the only type of partner a dynamic man like Ross could be.

"But you would consider a silent partner, someone who'd put up the money and leave the rest to you?" he pressed.

Wasn't that why she'd gone to the bank to try to secure a loan? "Well, yes."

He regarded her wordlessly, looking for a minute as if he was struggling with his own doubts about the wisdom of plunging ahead. But in the end, he said bluntly, "That's more or less what I'm proposing. I'm offering to put up the money, control the books..."

Control. Her mind fastened on the word and worried over it. Her fingers curled around the napkin in her lap, nervously pleating the fabric. She met his gaze. "I need to do things my way."

"Within reason, I don't find that a problem." He leaned back as the waitress set a large wooden bowl filled with crisp greens, and two salad plates on the table.

Within reason. What did that mean? Aware he was watching her, Linda helped herself to some salad, and ladled on the ranch dressing. "When would you find that a problem?" she asked, her look direct and uncompromising.

Ross carefully dished lettuce onto his plate. "When something doesn't make sense from a business standpoint. Suppose, for instance, you were using a supplier that gave you a forty percent break off retail, when you could easily use a supplier who might give you a forty-two percent break on the same products. I know it doesn't sound like very much, but at the end of the year those pennies add up. That's where I come in. I'd make details like that work for a client, rather than against them."

"You're a perfectionist." A trait, in her mind, that was disastrous where preschoolers were concerned. With small children, one had to be flexible, accepting. At the moment, Ross seemed anything but. On the other hand, he had handled his four-year-old daughter with a sure, loving manner. Not too strict. And the preschool was run for children just like Kimberly.

"When it comes to business, yes, I am a perfectionist."

She wondered briefly if there would be any pleasing him. She was silent, mulling over the problems and possibilities, trying to figure him out. "Why would you want to do this for me?" she asked finally. She couldn't believe his reasons were completely altruistic, and he was enough of a business person to know that the profits in a child-care business were never very large. In fact, to keep the costs affordable for parents, preschools were often run just above the red, which would have been a problem for her had she been interested in making money.

"The most important thing in the world to me is my daughter," he admitted, his gaze fixed on her unblinkingly. "I want her safe and happy. I have a full-time housekeeper, but Kimberly is at a point in her life when she needs more than Mrs. Delancey. She needs a place to go to school while I'm at work, a place where she'll be happy and well cared for, a place where she can learn how to interact with other children. Over the past three weeks I've talked to scores of people and visited thirty some schools in the area. Many of them were completely unacceptable for Kimberly."

So he was a perfectionist in that regard, too, she thought uncomfortably.

Ross continued pragmatically, his unhappiness with the situation evident. "The schools that are good have waiting lists at least two years long."

"I know," Linda replied, unhappy with the facts, too. She felt quality education and child-care ought to be readily available to children everywhere.

"Of every place we visited, Kimberly liked your school the best, and so did I."

"So you're doing this so she'll have a place in my school?" In other words, he was trying to buy Kimberly's way in, in the only way he could. Linda wasn't sure how she felt about that. On the one hand it was incredibly presumptuous and controlling, on the other hand incredibly caring.

Ross also didn't deny his true motives, and Linda had always respected honesty.

Nonetheless, she wondered at the depth of his interest in the Harrigan Enrichment Center. Would he maintain his financial support over the long haul, or just until his daughter no longer needed the preschool?

"But that's not the only reason," Ross continued easily, sensing she was about to protest. "I'm also a businessman and I know a good investment when I see one. Your school will succeed. All you need is the money and chance to build an engaging, stimulating curriculum as you see fit."

As they started on their entrées—steak for him and chicken teriyaki for her—she said, "I admit what you're offering is enticing. In fact, almost too good to be true. But this isn't as simple as you're trying to make it out to be. A partnership could get sticky."

While she was doubtful, he exuded confidence. "We'll spell everything out in writing first. Split the profits fifty-fifty."

She had to admit that sounded fair. She'd half expected him to expect a sixty/forty split in his favor, because he was taking the bulk of the financial risk.

"But we don't even know each other."

He lifted his hands and let them fall, as if it were of no consequence. "That, too, can be remedied easily enough. We'll get to know one another over time. We'll agree to deal with one another directly, without dancing around one another's feelings unnecessarily."

Linda was finding she couldn't argue with much of anything he'd said. Already she was dreaming of what his offer meant, the things she could do, the additional children she could teach. And that dream alone was enough to tempt her to take the risk. "I'd have a lot of requirements of my own," she began sternly, already knowing in her heart she was going to at least try to make this business deal work out.

"I expected as much." He looked at her seriously. "And I—"

"Mr. Hollister?" a male voice interrupted. They both looked up to see a bow-tied waiter hovering at their elbow. "There's a phone call for you. If you'll please come this way—"

Linda watched as a perplexed Ross strode off to take the call. He returned moments later, looking grim. He said, his expression troubled, "It's Kimberly—an emergency. I'm sorry but I have to go."

Chapter Two

"Would you mind if we dropped by my place first?" Ross asked. They were both walking hurriedly, Linda struggling to keep up with his pace. "I can take you home after that."

"Sure," Linda agreed, sliding in. Earlier, he'd been so busy paying the bill there'd been no opportunity to ask for details. "What's the problem, or shouldn't I ask?" She didn't want to pry. On the other hand, if she was going to be walking into some calamity, she wanted to be prepared.

Ross tugged at the knot of his tie, and for a brief moment looked faintly embarrassed. "Well, I guess... You're a preschool teacher—you'll understand. Know how these things are. Kimberly's lost her teddy bear, and according to Mrs. Delancey, she's inconsolable." He grimaced. "Kimberly can go into tantrums."

Linda looked at him in sympathy. She knew that very dependent children required special treatment. "Has this ever happened before?"

"Yes, once in a while I get a call and have to race home." Ross frowned. "But she's never been this frantic. It may be just that she didn't have a nap today and is overtired. It may be the move, which I know was traumatic for her. She left the only home she's ever known and came to a new state. She's encountered some culture shock." Linda blinked, and he elaborated dryly, "Cowboys, pickups, armadillos in the road, lizards on the patio, mariachi music. None of that is very Philadelphia-esque."

"Oh, yes, I see your point," she faltered.

"And I've had to be away a lot, too, at work." Regret laced his low tone. "I have a feeling it's all caught up with her tonight. Losing Bear was just the last straw. Anyway, I promised Mrs. Delancey I'd come home right away." His jaw took on a determined tilt and he finished pragmatically, "Hopefully, we'll locate Bear, I can calm Kimberly down and put her to bed, and then we can finish our discussion over coffee." He slanted her a questioning glance. "Is that all right with you?"

Linda nodded. Although at first she'd had her doubts, Ross seemed to have a handle on the crisis at home. What was more, he was sensitive to the feelings of others—his daughter's, hers. "That'd be fine," Linda said.

Because he still seemed concerned about not inconveniencing or upsetting her unduly, she gave him a reassuring smile. He smiled back. In the brief second their eyes met and held, she thought again what a nice, capable man he was, how at peace with himself and the world around him. Yes, there were problems—problems he readily acknowledged—but he met them all calmly, with a thinking man's precision.

Moments later, they pulled up at a white stone, two-story house in Northwest Hills. Built on the top of a slope, it had a great view of the city and the rolling, tree-covered hills beyond. Black shutters adorned the windows, the wooden trim was slate blue. The house and landscaped yard both looked well tended.

A tearful Kimberly greeted them at the door. "Daddy, I can't find Bear!" She was dressed in a Strawberry Shortcake nightgown. Her eyes were red and puffy from crying.

"We've looked everywhere for him," a plump, pleasant-looking gray-haired woman said. Clearly, she was at wit's end.

Sliding an arm around Linda's waist to draw her forward, Ross introduced Mrs. Delancey to Linda. As the two women exchanged hellos, Ross bent down to his daughter. Without further ado, he gathered her up in his arms and brushed the tangled damp blond hair from her eyes. "Okay, let's start from the very beginning. Where and when did you last see Bear?" he asked seriously, in a soft, sympathetic tone.

"I don't know." Kimberly sniffed helplessly, rubbing a fist alongside her eye. She looked at her daddy, her chin quivering, her green eyes devoid of all hope of ever regaining her cherished Bear. "I c-can't remember."

Ross frowned thoughtfully and patted her back in a soothing, reassuring manner. "I know you had him this afternoon."

"She took him to the grocery store earlier," Mrs. Delancey put in, eager to help solve the mystery. "Remember?"

Ross groaned, thinking about what that might mean.

"Oh, no—" Kimberly cried, immediately even more distraught. "I hope I didn't leave him in the grocery!"

"No, I'm sure you didn't," Ross said bolsteringly for Kimberly's benefit. "You know, the more I think about it, I'm sure you didn't leave Bear at the store, honey. We would have noticed he was missing before now if we had." He continued to pat his daughter on the shoulder, silently telling her everything was going to be all right. To Mrs. Delancey, he said, "Where have you looked?"

She sighed wearily. "Literally everywhere."

"We've been searching for an hour!" Kimberly cried again, clearly exhausted.

"Almost," Mrs. Delancey confirmed with a sigh and a glance at her watch. She glanced back at Kimberly, clearly hoping for a solution soon, or her heart would break right along with Kimberly's.

What they needed here was reason, cool logical thinking from someone with a clear head who wasn't emotionally involved, Linda thought. "Is there any way I can help?" she asked Ross impulsively, not wanting to intrude, but knowing the sooner they found Kimberly's bear the better. And Ross was right, Bear was probably somewhere in the house. Maybe even right under their noses.

"Sure." Ross looked grateful for all and any help.

Relieved to be of some assistance, and not just standing around idle while everyone searched, Linda asked, "Where should I start?"

"Here would be fine." Ross gestured at the living room, a room that was both child-proofed and homey. Plump throw pillows were scattered across the back of the plaid sofa, along with a coordinating navy-and-white hand-knit afghan. There were books and magazines galore, telling Linda that Ross was a very literate man, and judging by the collection of children's storybooks there, she could see he intended for his daughter to be the same. She noted he had a moderately priced stereo system and extensive collection of records and cassettes, some looking as if they might date back to his college days. Several toys were scattered about the room—including a Candyland game, crayons and coloring book, another doll, and a half-built tower of blocks. The toy chest in the corner was brimming over. And there were a number of children's records and cassettes in the built-in bookshelves beside the white stone fireplace. "Look anywhere he might have fallen," Ross counseled.

"I've already checked under all the furniture," Mrs. Delancey said, wringing her hands as she followed Ross and Kimberly up the carpeted stairs.

The next ten minutes were consumed with quiet searching. Downstairs alone, Linda looked behind the sofa, under the chairs, behind the draperies, in the magazine racks and under the newspaper.

By the time she reached the kitchen, Kimberly had trailed back downstairs, Mrs. Delancey following. "Would you mind if I looked in the kitchen cupboards?" Linda asked. Having given up on the visual approach, she was now trying to go about this logically—putting herself in the place of a precocious four-year-old, trying to figure out where Kimberly might want Bear to "visit."

"Be my guest," Mrs. Delancey smiled, looking faintly mystified. "Though what Bear would be doing there..."

But Bear wasn't in the cupboards, as it turned out, nor was he in the dining room. Looking faintly anxious and perplexed himself, Ross came back downstairs. "Maybe we should switch floors," he said wearily, obviously hoping a change of locations would do the trick. "I'll search the first floor, if you ladies'll take the second."

"Sure," Linda said amiably. Privately she was curious about the rest of his house, now that she'd seen the downstairs. Would his bedroom be decorated as cozily and masculinely as the living room? Or would it be furnished in some floral motif his wife had picked out years ago, and that for practical or sentimental reasons he had never bothered to replace? He certainly seemed to have adjusted to the life of a single parent; but on the other hand he exhibited none of the outgoing charm of a single man on the prowl.

Shaking off her musings, she turned her attention to the matter at hand. Maybe if she personally helped Kimberly look for her bear, working together as a team, they might have better success.

"Kimberly," she asked the teary little girl gently, "do you want to show me where your room is? Maybe if we look together we can find Bear."

Kimberly studied Linda a moment, then finally deciding she could trust her to partake in this very serious search, nodded slowly. "Okay."

Shuffling along the carpet determinedly, Kimberly led the way upstairs to her room. As Linda had expected, the little girl's private sanctuary was decorated prettily and filled with toys, stuffed animals and plenty of books. A child-sized easel stood in one corner, a comfortable adult rocker in another. On the table beside the bed was a framed photo. Looking at it, Linda froze.

"That's my mommy," Kimberly said, picking up the picture. She showed it to Linda. "Wasn't she pretty?"

Yes, Ross's wife had been pretty, Linda thought. Tiny and blond. Cheerful. She was holding a two-year-old Kimberly in her arms. Both were dressed in sundresses and sandals.

Linda gave the photo back to Kimberly, who replaced it reverently on the bedstand.

With sublime effort Linda turned her attention back to the search. She tried to stifle the questions that flooded through her.

"Do you like my room?" Kimberly asked.

Linda nodded. "Oh, yes. I love it. And you have a very pretty canopy bed!"

"I like it, too!" Kimberly exclaimed. "I feel just like a princess when I sleep in it."

Linda grinned. "I know what you mean. I had a bed like that when I was little, too." And she had felt like a princess.

Trying to figure out a place where Bear could have slipped out of sight, Linda moved closer to the bed, which was almost flush against the wall. Meanwhile, Kimberly was down on her hands and knees, lifting up the pink dust ruffle. "Nothing under the bed," she said, and sneezed.

"Except a little dust," Linda teased, as she got down on her knees, scanned the area, found nothing, and sneezed, too.

Then, on a whim, she climbed up on the bed, and peered down into the tiny narrow space between mattress and wall. She almost missed it—a tiny speck of brown, a glimpse of a battered ear sticking up. The stuffed animal was indeed wedged securely between the mattress and the wall. "Hmm, I wonder how this got here." Linda lifted it out. She turned to Kimberly. "Is this Bear?"

Relief flooding her cherubic features, Kimberly rushed forward and grabbed Bear. She held him to her chest, burying her face in his plump brown tummy. "Bear," she murmured, exhaling on a contented sigh.

"Come on." Linda smiled and held out a hand to Kimberly. "Let's go tell your daddy what we found."

"Thank goodness!" Ross said, relieved.

Kimberly yawned. "Sleepy?" Ross asked.

She nodded. Still clutching Bear, she edged closer to him and leaned against him. "It's time for my bedtime story."

Ross looked at Linda questioningly. "Do you mind?"

Linda knew it would be better if Ross put Kimberly to bed himself. But aware they hadn't finished their discussion, she said, "Not at all. I'll be downstairs when you're ready to talk."

In a way she was glad they had suffered this crisis. It gave her an opportunity to see Ross in action; she liked the way his personality seemed to blossom under fire, the fact he'd been able to stay calm, and gentle with his daughter, throughout the ordeal.

Maybe he was the right person to finance the expansion of her preschool, after all; he certainly seemed to understand and appreciate small children—their fears and traumas, their limited view of life, and their complete emotional dependency on those closest to them.

Visibly relieved the calamity was over, Mrs. Delancey smiled and said, "I'll put on a pot of coffee."

While Linda waited for the coffee to brew, she took another surreptitious look around the living room. Not surprisingly, there were no photos of Ross's wife. The questions about the pretty blond woman in the picture rushed back in force. Was he still in love with her? And what had happened to her? Were they divorced?

When Ross came back downstairs twenty minutes later, Linda was ensconced in the family room before the television set, a cup of coffee in hand. "Mrs. Delancey said to tell you she'll be in her room if you need her," she reported dutifully.

Ross poured himself some coffee from the carafe on the tray. "Poor woman—she must be exhausted."

Mrs. Delancey had looked tired, Linda thought. As did Ross now. "How's Kimberly?" she asked gently.

"Asleep."

Linda imagined how precious Kimberly must look in sleep, all curled up in that delightful canopy bed. She was such a beautiful child, so bright and active. It was easy to see why Ross doted on her so much, and why Kimberly sometimes felt like a princess. And yet that wasn't an entirely healthy experience, Linda felt. Because too much protection as a child could lead to an unwillingness to risk, to venture out, as an adult. The tantrums were a symptom. She, Linda, knew that better than anyone. "She depends a lot on Bear," Linda said finally, when it seemed he was waiting for her to make some remark.

Ross nodded. "Yes. Bear's her security blanket," he admitted softly. His green eyes darkened, looking faintly troubled. "He's become even more important to her since we moved." Ross took a lengthy sip of his coffee.

To Linda that was easily explained. Bear was one of the few constants in Kimberly's dramatically changed world. She wondered what other changes Kimberly had recently coped with, and again what had happened to Kimberly's mother.

"Is Mrs. Delancey new?" she asked.

He stretched his long legs out in front of him in a relaxed manner and pressed his spine more comfortably against the back of the sofa. Although she was sitting several feet away from him, on the other sofa, she was suddenly aware of the rich mossy scent of his after-shave. The fireplace opposite them was empty, and she found herself wondering if he ever enjoyed a fire in the evenings. Maybe after Kimberly was in bed and Mrs. Delancey had retired he would sit in front of the red and blue flames, dim the lights and turn on the stereo...

His voice interrupted her thoughts which had meandered into dangerous territory.

"No, she's not new. Mrs. Delancey's been with us since my wife's death, when Kimberly was two."

He gave her a minute to soak that in, then his eyes met hers candidly. "I wouldn't have made the move south if Mrs. Delancey hadn't agreed to go with us, promotion or no."

Linda felt sad. Both Ross and Kimberly had suffered a tragic loss recently. The knowledge only increased her admiration for his commitment to his daughter.

"No, that's part of the problem." Ross frowned unhappily. He sat up a little straighter and raked a hand through his hair. "You see, I think I might have overprotected her unknowingly. When Karen died I could've put her in a day-care center, but I didn't want to do that. It was enough, her losing her mother, without having to adjust to that, too."

For a second, there was a hitch of pain in his voice as he talked about his loss, but then he recovered and went on, "So I hired a housekeeper instead. And although Kimberly went to the park to play, she didn't get out nearly as often as she had when Karen was alive. Especially during the winter months. Without my realizing it, Kimberly became more and more shy." He sighed. "The move to unfamiliar surroundings has just exacerbated this. That's why I'm so determined to get her into a school program with a caring teacher before she begins kindergarten. I want her to be able to handle the social aspects of school, before she's thrown into the academics. And from what I understand, they start reading in kindergarten now?" He found that a bit daunting.

Linda was touched by all that he revealed. She remembered she herself hadn't learned her numbers and letters until first grade. Linda smiled. "In Texas, they do. Of course we have full-day kindergarten here, too, which is still an anomaly in some states. But I think it's a positive step. The advent of television, the beginning of programs like *Sesame Street* and *Electric*

Company and *Mr. Rogers*, made children more ready for school than you or I were."

Ross leaned back against the cushions and stretched his long legs out in front of him. He shook his head in a way that told her he felt like Rip Van Winkle. "I feel like I've been negligent, not doing something about her education sooner."

From what Linda had seen, Ross had nothing to apologize for. "Kimberly will catch up," she soothed. "And she'll adjust even if she doesn't go to preschool, although I think enrolling her in at least a part-time program is an excellent idea. It'll help Kimberly later if she learns to handle group dynamics now. She'll learn how to participate, lead, and work as a member of a team."

His head lifted. His gaze narrowed in on her face as he paused, his cup halfway to his lips before he put it down again to rest against one gently braced, muscular thigh. Reluctantly she tore her eyes away from his leg and returned her eyes to his, and saw the hope, the taut anticipation on his face.

"Have you decided if you're going to take me up on my offer of a partnership?" he questioned bluntly, anxiously. So much was riding on this. His future, Linda's, Kimberly's...

Yes, Linda thought, she had. But aloud she said, "I'd like to look into the possibility." She was still determined to proceed with caution.

"So where do we begin?" He looked at her, leaning forward to pour himself more coffee. Now that she'd said maybe, he was all business again. "Shall I have my lawyer draw up a contract?"

Linda nodded. She would take it to her attorney and to her sister-in-law, Diana, to read. If anything at all was amiss, Diana would spot it in an instant. If it wasn't, they would have a deal.

GLENNA ARRIVED FOR WORK bright and early the following morning. Once a week she and Linda got together early for a lesson-planning session an hour before school started. Linda always fixed the coffee and Glenna brought the doughnuts.

"Rough night, huh?" Glenna said, taking a good look at her boss under the kitchen lights.

Linda grinned wryly. Glenna didn't pull any punches with her comments. That was one of the things Linda liked best about her. Peering closer, she noted there were faint circles under Glenna's brown eyes, which lacked their usual sparkle, and her bobbed, carrot-colored hair had not been carefully blow-dried as usual. "You don't look like you're in the best of form, either," Linda noted.

Glenna sighed. "True. But you go first. What happened to make you lose sleep?"

"I was up late last night 'negotiating.'"

"And?" Glenna said, setting the eclectic mix of frosted doughnuts out on a plate.

"We may have financial backing for expanding our center."

Glenna cried out and grabbed Linda in a quick embrace. "Tell me about it."

Linda did as Glenna selected a chocolate doughnut and took a seat at the kitchen table.

"Now it's your turn to 'fess up," Linda prodded good-naturedly when she'd finished. "What's causing your loss of sleep?"

Glenna put both elbows on the table and glumly rested her chin in her hands. "Need you even ask? It's Martin again. I tell you, this business of getting married is giving me nothing but grief!"

It wasn't any wonder to Linda that the recently engaged couple were under stress. They'd only given themselves a little over a month to plan the event. Now almost a week had passed, and Glenna had done little but pick out a dress, and secure a chapel near the campus. Meanwhile, Martin, who was also a summer graduate of the University of Texas, was busily settling into his new job as an engineer. He'd managed to rent a tux, but that was all.

"What's he done this time?" Linda asked sympathetically.

Glenna sighed and used a napkin to wipe some chocolate off her hand. "We just can't agree on anything about the wedding. We were up until after one last night discussing the guest list. He wants to keep it to fifty. Whereas my parents are insisting we have at least two hundred guests on our side alone."

Linda made a mock sound of pain. "Can't you compromise?"

"That's what we did." Glenna decided on another doughnut, this one jelly-filled. "We decided on one hundred."

"So?" Linda sensed there was more.

"So, I don't know what I'm going to tell my sorority sisters who aren't going to be invited, many of whom are still in town."

Linda grinned. "You'll think of something."

"I hope so. Or I'm telling you I am dead meat!"

Having talked out their problems, the two women got down to business, planning the lessons for the following week. They were just cleaning up when the doorbell rang, announcing the arrival of their first student of the day. Glenna went to get it.

Seconds later, Tad raced in. Gregarious as usual, he gave Linda and Glenna both welcoming hugs. "Hi, everybody!" he shouted exuberantly.

"Hi, Tad," Linda said, affectionately ruffling his soft and shiny black hair. "How are you today?"

"Great! Wanna see my frog?"

"Not a real one, I hope," Linda said, as he reached into the pocket of his immaculately pressed khaki shorts. Stranger things had happened. Once, one of the kids had brought in a live chameleon he'd caught, zipped in his jacket pocket.

"Nope. It's made out of dough, see?" He held up an unrecognizable lump of clay. Still soft, it had been mushed out of shape by spending time in his pocket.

"Mommy made me this stuff last night, out of flour and salt, and food coloring and water! It was really, really neat. I've been playing with it all morning!"

"That's wonderful, Tad. Maybe you can share it with the class during Show and Tell this morning!" Especially interesting to them would be the way his mother had made the modeling clay from scratch.

During the exchange, Tad's mother, Wendy, had been standing patiently by. When the first opening in the conversation came, she said hello and asked to talk to Linda privately.

"Sure," Linda said. "Glenna?"

"Tad, come on. You can help me set up the tables. We're going to do finger painting later this morning."

"We are! Neato!"

Linda led Wendy into the adjoining computer lab, where they could have a little privacy. "What can I do for you?" she asked. A pretty woman in her late twenties, Wendy generally had the perpetually harassed look of a newly single parent, but this morning her face was glowing with excitement. "I have some great news and I just wanted to tell you. I've decided to go for my real-estate license, and I've been offered a salaried position as a trainee by one of the local realtors. They're paying my tuition in a comprehensive three-week course that starts next Monday. Then I'll be able to take the exam and get my license."

Linda understood Wendy's excitement. One of Wendy's main problems to date had been the lack of a marketable job skill. Currently she was clerking in a dry-cleaning store for minimum wage, and relying on her musician ex-husband for child support. Linda knew from things both Tad and Wendy had said to her that they just barely managed to scrape by, but at least they loved each other and generally made the most of every moment together. Tad's one lament was that he didn't ever get to see much of his father, who was out of town a lot.

"Well, I think that's wonderful," Linda said, smiling at Wendy. "It sounds like a terrific opportunity."

"It is. I'm just a little worried about the studying aspect of it. There's so much to learn—all that math, and all those terms like *escrow*. I've been out of school for so long, seven years now, and you know I never did more than finish high school."

"Trust me," Linda said soothingly. "Studying gets easier when you get older. Mostly because you're more focused. You can do it."

"Well, I'm going to give it my best shot," Wendy said. She glanced at her watch. "Gosh, I've got to go." Not wanting to be late for work, she quickly said her goodbyes to Linda, Glenna and Tad and then dashed out.

Soon after, three-year-old Dexter charged in. Not the patient sort, he immediately tried to get into the thick of things. "Dexter, no," Glenna said, when he tried to open one of the jars of paint she had set out on the tables. "We're not going to paint just yet."

"Why not? I'm ready." Dexter said, pulling up a chair and plopping down on it with a petulant frown.

"Dexter, I need someone to pass out our painting smocks and put one on each of the chairs. Do you think you can do that for me?" Linda said.

Dexter cannoned out of the chair. "Sure I can!" Marching forward importantly, he prepared to assume the task.

Watching Dexter work, Glenna whispered to Linda, out of earshot of the children who had arrived, "You know I still think Dexter might be hyperactive."

There was no doubt he was active. But as for him being abnormally so, to Linda, the tag just didn't fit. "I think he'll be all right once he settles in here," she said to her younger associate. "But you're right, sometimes he can tax the patience." Matters weren't helped by the attitude of his parents who, at least from what Linda had seen, did not impose limits of any kind on their son.

Glenna was about to argue when the bell rang again. "Oh, well, duty calls," she said. The rest of the morning was uneventful. Or relatively so. Dexter, in his eagerness to get to the painting, spilled nearly half a jar on the table and himself, lending a rather tie-dyed effect to his clothes. Fortunately the paint was washable and would come out. But it was a mess, one neither Linda nor Glenna enjoyed cleaning up.

They were glad when it was time for the kids to take their morning break outdoors. And that was when Ross stopped by. "I just spent the morning with my attorney," he stated as soon as they were seated comfortably in her living room. "He has advised me that we should sign a dissolution agreement as part of the partnership papers."

Linda's lawyer—recommended by her sister-in-law—had mentioned that, too, but fearing it would jinx their whole project from the start, she had acted on gut instinct and refused. She looked at the calm but determined expression on his face and emitted a weary sigh. She should have known, conventional man that Ross was, he would opt for the safest course.

"Do you really think we need it?" she asked, exasperated, hoping he'd relent.

He nodded, firm on his resolve. "Yes," he replied implacably. "I think it's appropriate to plan now what we would do if we ever had to break up our partnership at any point in the future. Furthermore, I think we should add a time frame to the agreement—give the partnership a renewable option of, say, a year. That way we'd have enough time to get the Center up and running, and the enrollment at anticipated levels.''

And what if they didn't? Linda wondered nervously. If they fell short of his goals, would he chuck everything? As much as she wanted to expand her business, she also wanted to see it survive. Unfortunately he did not have the same need, for Kimberly would be in kindergarten in the public school in another year. And no longer her student.

"What happens after one year?" she asked, her voice faltering slightly. She wanted him to spell out precisely what he planned to do the day their original contract was up.

Ross shrugged noncommittally. "It depends on where we are. If the financial picture is okay and you don't need me, I may bow out and just let you run the show. If not, we decide where we are and if we want to continue, then we renew the same contract on option, or draw up a new one. Whatever."

His words were laced with common sense, but Linda still felt shell-shocked.

Apparently sensing she still needed some persuading, he continued, "An open-ended contract isn't in either of our best interests. We need to make this more specific than a general, handshake deal. In fact, the more specific the entire partnership agreement is, the better." He seemed convinced their signing would help them avoid future pitfalls.

Linda, however, wasn't so sure. "I see." Needing some time to sort out her feelings, Linda got up and walked back into the part of her home that served as the main classroom. Outside, the sounds of the children playing punctuated the silence. She picked up several plastic jars of paint and carried them to the adjacent storeroom. She needed to get the finger-painting mess cleaned up before the students filtered back in for their lesson on France.

He followed, watching as she set the paint on the appropriate shelf. "You're hurt," he guessed.

She pivoted, her back against the shelf. Her chin lifted with a small measure of defiance. "I suppose I am." She was also no longer as sure of him.

He studied her briefly, then continued on resolutely, "I think we should name an arbitrator, someone to settle any disputes that might come up between us."

"What kind of disputes?" Linda demanded irately. Then remembering her mother's adage about catching more flies with honey than vinegar, she said sweetly, "If you're just handling the books, and I'm handling the school, what could come up?"

He grinned, recognizing the Southern Belle tone. He gave her a tolerant glance. "It's just a formality, Linda. A safeguard."

"It sounds to me like you're having second thoughts already, Ross," she accused bluntly, wanting him to be totally honest with her, with himself. "Are you?" If so, she needed to know—now! She had been married to a man who wasn't supportive of her goals. She wouldn't get involved with Ross if their partnership repeated that disaster.

"No." He gave her an emphatic look, implying she was wrong not to trust him.

"Well, now I'm beginning to have doubts," Linda said flatly, all the former enthusiasm drained from her face. He gave her an accusing look, which in turn prompted her to explain her feelings. "I know one year sounds adequate, but in reality it's an awfully short amount of time to get everything going. We have no staff, and mountains of work."

"But you and Glenna aren't in this alone," he countered. "I'm in it, too, and I'll help you—both of you, however you need me to help. I promise."

She could see he meant what he said. "All right," she said finally, then impetuously added a condition of her own: "But I want the option to buy you out at the end of one year written into the contract, too."

As she took charge of the situation, she began to think positively once again. "After all, if things are going well and I've proved myself as a manager and educator of a full-sized facility, I'll be able to get a bank loan by then. I'll use the school as collateral."

He nodded, relief softening his features slightly. "Consider it done. I'll have my lawyer get on it first thing."

That decided, they concluded their meeting and she started to show him to the door. He paused at the portal and turned back to her. His voice dropped to a low, reassuring pitch. His gaze was kind but serious. "Everything is going to work out, Linda. I just have the feeling."

She knew it would too, even if she had to move heaven and earth.

"SO WHERE DO I SIGN?" Linda asked with only faint feelings of trepidation the following Wednesday evening at seven-thirty.

"Right here on the dotted line," Ross said happily, handing her a pen.

They were at her home. Both their attorneys were present. Though she signed her name, she had to suppress her anxiety, the feeling she was on the edge of a precipice.

The lawyers departed, leaving Linda and Ross alone at the big table in her kitchen.

"Well, partner, how does it feel?" he asked, leaning back in his chair. She couldn't help but note that the jacket of his suit was still buttoned.

"It feels good," she said carefully. But scary. She'd just signed papers that would give them enough operating capital to rent space for approximately forty-eight children and four classrooms. She and Ross hoped to eventually expand the school to seventy-two children in six classrooms.

He glanced at his watch. "I know you have to teach tomorrow, and I've got to work. But there's space in several buildings we should look at."

Now that they'd signed the papers and made it official, Linda, too, felt the pressure to get started, even though they'd originally had no plans to do anything concrete until the weekend when both were free. "Where are they?"

"One is off Route 183, just north of Balcones. The other is on McNeil Road. There's another on Parmer Lane."

He really had done his homework, Linda realized, stunned by the no-holds-barred way he'd thrown himself into the venture. Trying to put her mind at ease, she told herself that it just proved she wouldn't have to handle everything alone.

"You want to go now?" she asked.

He nodded. "Just give me a minute to make a few calls to the leasing agents."

Minutes later they were on their way. To their mutual disappointment, however, the first two locations were inadequate. Neither had yards, and Linda rejected them on sight. The third, however, was an existing day-care center that had been closed down when the original center relocated to larger quarters. There were six classrooms—each equipped with a sink, child-sized restrooms, and a kitchen. The fenced-in backyard, however, had no playground equipment. A nice feature on the other hand was its convenience to both their homes—hers in Spicewood and his in Northwest Hills ten minutes away.

"It needs a lot of work inside," Linda murmured, studying the concrete walls and stained rugs with a practical eye.

He nodded. "New carpet, paint."

"Plus we'll need shelves for all the toys." Suddenly it seemed like an awful lot of work. Linda pushed away the nagging sensation she'd taken on more than she could handle. This would work out. She just had to be patient, not expect too much of herself too soon. Or of Ross, either.

With paper and pen, she began taking inventory of changes that would have to be made if they chose this site. Forcing herself to look on the bright side, Linda said, "Of course we won't have to buy everything. I can move what's in my home over here. The playground equipment, too."

Ross, too, studied the rundown interior, seeing not what it was then, but what it could be. "Even utilizing what you've already got, we'll still need a lot more furniture, equipment and toys, but it shouldn't take too long to get them, a couple of weeks maybe." He turned to her quizzically. "Assuming we can manage to get everything ordered and delivered. Do you think we can get licensed in that amount of time?"

Linda nodded slowly. "I'll manage. My biggest problem will be finding another teacher on such short notice who has a degree in early-childhood education or child development." She wanted the best staff possible. And that took not only hard work and painstaking interviews, but time.

His light brows drew together worriedly, as the next thought hit. "Have you talked to the wait-listed people yet?"

"All are agreeable to enrolling as soon as we expand. So, including Kimberly, we'll have eleven new students right away. Not counting any others we get to sign up in the meantime."

He looked as pleased about that as she was, and they shared a brief smile. "Good. The sooner we open the better."

Her hands on her hips, Linda strolled about the room thoughtfully, her high heels making clicking noises on the scuffed linoleum floor. "I agree. I think we've found our new Center."

Ross strode up to her with his hand extended. She took it in hers, ignoring the warm charge that ran through her. "Congratulations," he said. Stepping back, he surveyed the room again and asked, "What should we call it? The Harrigan-Hollister Enrichment Center?"

Linda was for a moment taken aback. She'd worked so hard to make the Harrigan Center that it was disturbing to her hard-won independence to link their names in public. She let it sit with her a moment, then turned to him, a glint in her eyes. "It does have a nice ring to it. Why not?"

"I SWEAR IF THAT MAN gives me one more order I'm going to scream," Glenna vowed, slamming down the phone.

Linda looked up from the bulletin board she was assembling for a classroom in the new building. Since the lease had been signed ten days ago, she and Glenna had worked at the new location every evening, getting things organized. Two hours nightly for them both, and entire weekends for Linda, didn't seem like a whole lot of time invested. And yet they had managed a tremendous amount. The new Center was looking better every day.

"Martin giving you grief again?" she asked sympathetically as she took another satisfied look at the new navy carpet and the freshly painted light blue walls.

"And then some," Glenna admitted sourly, throwing down her pen, and abandoning the student rosters she had been working on. She ticked off her complaints about her mate-to-be with increasing vigor. "You know, he hasn't done anything to prepare for our wedding, except arrange for his tux?" She tapped her chest dramatically. "I've had to call the minister, order the flowers, address the invitations!" She held up her hand, staving off any interruption from her boss. "I know, I know. Most of this is the responsibility of the bride and/or her family, but that's not the way we agreed to work it!" Glenna stormed. "We agreed when we set the wedding date that we'd divide the work equally."

"And he hasn't lived up to his end of the bargain," Linda said as she finished cutting out a construction paper tree for her bulletin board.

"He hasn't even tried!" Glenna said. She paced over to the window and stood looking out at the newly sodded play yard. Hands on her hips, she said, "Honestly, sometimes I think he just wants me to chuck it all and run off and elope!"

Linda raised an inquiring brow. "Do you?"

"Yes. No. I don't know." Glenna buried her face in her hands. Just that quickly, all the fight left her. She was limp, exhausted, ready to give in.

Uttering a ragged sigh, Glenna peered up at Linda through the fingers spread across her face. "I'm getting overemotional again, aren't I?" With the back of one hand, she wiped a few stray tears from her cheeks.

Linda put down her work and crossed the room to Glenna's side. Placing an arm about her shoulders, she said gently, "You're entitled to get a little crazy. Trying to put together a wedding can be very fretful."

And Linda knew just how Glenna felt because putting together a new preschool had been just as complicated. The past two weeks were the busiest Linda had ever spent. She worked all day with the children, evenings and weekends on preparations for the new school. Glenna was there about half the time. Ross a little more. To Linda's relief, they got along fine. In fact her feelings were beginning to worry her. She'd managed to hold in check her attraction to Ross. Her first order of business was establishing the school. She'd just have to keep trying to remain businesslike.

But what should she do about Glenna, who looked as if she were handling about double the stress she was able to tolerate? "Glenna, maybe you should just call it a day and go home. Rest."

"No, I'll be fine." Glenna shook off the suggestion adamantly. She headed back for the table where she'd been working. "Besides, I couldn't sleep now anyway. I'd just be thinking about Martin." She looked as if she was going to cry again. She picked up the stack of papers and thumped it deliberately. "What I need to do is just get back to work, get my mind off the wedding for a little while. Then maybe... maybe I'll be able to deal with all those details."

"I'm sorry the expansion of the Center is coming at such a bad time for you," Linda said.

"Don't be," Glenna assured her. "I think it's exciting. Ross is nice. And we have ten new students—eleven if you count Kimberly." She smiled, just thinking about it.

Linda grinned back. "Anxious to have your own class?" At present, Glenna was working under Linda's supervision. In the future, she would be doing her own lesson plans, taking on more responsibility, making more of her own decisions.

"You bet." Glenna looked down at her class roster and frowned. "I just wish..."

"What?" Linda prodded, sensing trouble.

Glenna shrugged. "That we could put Dexter in your class and Tad in mine."

"I wish so, too, but since we decided to separate three- and four-year-olds, we really don't have any choice. I have to take the four-year-olds because Ross insists Kimberly be in my class."

"Which leaves me the three-year-olds and the new teacher, Helen Masterson, the four-and-a-half-year-olds."

Linda studied the younger teacher carefully. "Is there a problem with you and Dexter?" Thus far, from everything she had seen, the two got along beautifully, even though the boy could be a handful.

"No. Dexter and I get along great. It's, well, I'm just not sure I can handle his parents. You know how flaky they are."

Linda nodded. Dexter's parents were both scholarly types who debated theories of every kind, including child-raising. Sometimes they voiced their opinions too assertively.

Realizing Linda understood, Glenna continued, "I'm afraid that what I think of them is more apparent than I want it to be." She hastened to add, "Not that I don't always try to be nice..."

"You don't have to apologize, Glenna. I have trouble talking to them too. Some of their theories aren't very realistic."

Encouraged, Glenna continued, "And don't you find it weird that his mother doesn't get upset about Dexter splattering his clothes with finger paint or marker? I mean, no matter what he's done, she never says a word."

"Well, the supplies we use are water-soluble," Linda said. "Maybe it's not a big problem."

"Oh, yeah, good point."

"But I know what you mean about Dexter," Linda continued warmly. "Sometimes at the end of the day he looks like he's been sifting through a garbage dump."

"And his mother never seems to mind. My mother would have had a fit if I'd ever come home from school looking that way."

Linda agreed. "Well, that's probably because she's used to it. According to our records, Dexter is the last child of six. And he's always been very precocious."

"True. I mean, he and Tad play together like equals, as if there's no difference in their ages."

"Yeah. A year's a lot at their age." Linda stapled indigo-blue background paper onto the bulletin board, adding, "Of course all that might change when we get the new students in. Both might find they have more in common with boys their own age."

Glenna nodded, looking reassured. They were all hoping for a smooth transition.

At that moment, the front door to the Center opened. Glenna's fiancé walked in, a tissue-wrapped bouquet of pink and white carnations clutched in his hand. An engineer for an Austin firm, Martin was dressed in khaki trousers, a plaid shirt buttoned to the neck, and a funky yellow tie decoratively emblazoned with question marks. Just twenty-two like Glenna, he wore his straight blond hair long, falling to the lower edge of his collar and over his ears. He wore wire-rimmed glasses and a properly apologetic look. "I'm sorry, sweetheart," he said, thrusting the flowers at Glenna. "I'm wrong and you were right. I should be more help."

"And I should be less of a grinch," Glenna sniffed, looking deliriously happy once again, now that the love of her life was near.

Linda smiled, wondering if she too would ever again feel that special way. "Go on, you two. Get out of here." She shooed them toward the door. "I'll finish up tonight."

"Are you sure?" Glenna asked.

"Positive. With just a little over a week to go to your wedding, you've both got tons of things to do to finish getting ready. Anything here can wait. Besides, the new staffer, Helen, is coming in tomorrow, and she's agreed to work overtime until the grand opening if need be. One way or another, everything will get done—even without your help."

"Thanks Linda." Glenna smiled. "I'll make this up to you and Ross, I promise."

Arm in arm, Glenna and Martin walked out the door just as Ross was walking in. He caught the happy look on Glenna's face, nodded, then focused on Linda who was stapling a vivid pink dinosaur onto the blue background of her bulletin board. He couldn't help but admire her silky smooth hands, as curvacious and lithe as the rest of her.

"Kimberly is so excited about coming to school here," he said, watching her put up more. "In fact that's all she talks about these days."

Linda smiled. "I'm glad," she said, continuing with her task. She knew the socializing and curriculum would be good for Kimberly, but wondered if Ross was prepared to deal with his daughter's feelings about leaving the security of her home.

"I'm glad you decided to teach and not just act as the school's director," Ross continued. "At least for now. I think it'll make the transition easier for Kimberly, since she likes you so much. And certainly the fact you'll be temporarily doing double duty will help the school out financially until we can get on our feet and offset some of the start-up costs for the new Center."

He was babbling now and knew it.

"I don't mind continuing to teach," Linda said. "Actually, leaving the classroom entirely is more than I could bear. Administrative work is okay, but I enjoy dealing with children a lot more. Also I want to get enrollment up before adding staff."

"Have you got the ads ready to run in the weekend papers?" Ross asked, studying her.

Linda nodded, suddenly aware she'd been staring at him absently, and that oddly enough, he hadn't seemed to mind. Feeling a little flustered, she rummaged around on her desk until she located the copies. A month ago, if anyone had told her she'd take in a business partner—never mind a handsome dynamic Yankee banker—she'd have told them they were crazy. And now here they were, their names publicly linked on the sign out front.

Aware a hint of embarrassed color was still in her cheeks, Linda motioned him over to her desk to view the ads.

Ross stood next to her—so close their shoulders were almost touching—and read over them leisurely. After what seemed to Linda to be an inordinate amount of time, his mouth crooked up approvingly. "You did a good job on these," he murmured. "They're very professional, but inviting, too."

"Thanks," Linda said evenly, aware that their closeness suddenly had a surreal quality to it, as if it were happening in a suspended moment of time and space. Her palms had started to perspire.

She moved a little farther back, without being obvious about her need to put space between them. "I don't think I left anything out."

His gaze was still on the ads. Finally he straightened and turned to face her. "I don't see anything, either. So what's next? Is there anything else you need me to get ready for the grand opening next week?"

Actually, he'd done far too much already.

"No, I think I can handle it from this point forward," she answered in her usual brisk tone.

In fact she would have to, she decided firmly, very much aware that her physical attraction to Ross was all wrong.

To work well with him, she had to remain emotionally uninvolved. And to do that, they had to remain as physically apart as possible—starting now.

Biting down on her new resolve, she led him to the front door.

"So I'll see you a little later," he said.

She nodded. But as she watched him stride down the sidewalk to his car, she wondered if she saw disappointment in his eyes, or whether it was just her imagination.

Chapter Three

Ross walked into the Center Monday morning at seven o'clock, Kimberly's hand tightly clutching his. He had known he would be nervous this first day of operation at the new location; he hadn't expected his daughter to be so anxious. He could see she was pale and worried, her tiny mouth flattened into an unhappy frown. It was the last thing he'd expected from her, today of all days. Especially since she'd had such a good time that day she had visited the Center when it was at Linda's home.

"You're going to have a good time today, Kimberly," Ross said, as he knelt and helped her off with her windbreaker. Other children were already playing with the toys.

Linda came toward them, looking fresh and pretty in an outdoorsy way. She'd swept her hair back off her face. She was wearing sneakers and white French canvas jeans, and a bright blue sweater with sparkling butterfly appliqués on the front. "Hi, Kimberly. Let me show you where your cubbyhole is, and the hook where you can hang your jacket." She started to reach for his daughter's hand.

Kimberly reacted negatively, turning and holding on to Ross with both hands. "My daddy will show me!" she said firmly, daring anyone to tell her otherwise.

Linda smiled. "I'd be glad to show you, Kimberly."

"No!" Kimberly said, holding on tighter to Ross's hand.

Linda looked at Ross expectantly. He knew what she wanted him to do—bid his farewell, and go, leaving her to handle Kimberly. She was worried that by giving in to Kimberly's truculent demands, he might be setting a terrible precedent, and guaranteeing similar temper tantrums every morning.

He sighed and looked down at his daughter. One look at her teary expression and he knew he couldn't leave. He had promised himself when Karen died that he wouldn't ever let a family member down again. He didn't care if people scorned him for being overprotective. Kimberly's happiness was what mattered here. She needed to feel secure. And he would stay until she was.

His decision made, he met Linda's searching gaze. "I'd like to show Kimberly around, if you don't mind."

He could tell by the faint darkening of Linda's eyes she disapproved of his decision. But she graciously allowed him the point. "All right. You know where her cubbyhole is. Kimberly's name is on everything."

Spying another parent and student coming in, Linda smiled and started for them.

Determined to reassure his daughter, Ross walked her around the classroom to which she was assigned, showing her where everything was stored, carefully admiring everything on the bulletin board. Other children were frolicking on the carpeted play area. Ross walked Kimberly over to the shelves, achingly aware she still had a death grip on his hand. His guilt over her shyness increased. This was all his fault, for not having gotten her out more. Just like Karen's death was his fault, if not directly, then indirectly.

Aware his daughter hadn't relaxed in the slightest, Ross did his best to put her at ease and get her mind off her fright. "Would you like to pick out a toy?" he asked.

"No, Daddy. I don't want to play. I want you to stay with me."

He held back a sigh. A surreptitious glance at the clock above told him that at this rate he was going to be late for work, and he had several important meetings to run this morning. Nonetheless, given the choice, his first priority had to be his daughter's happiness, no matter how much hardship it caused him later. "How about the blocks?" Ross persisted, thinking if he could just get her involved in some activity everything would be okay. Kimberly loved to build block towers.

"No!"

"The matchbox cars?"

"No."

A little girl in a frilly pink dress came up beside them. She smiled at Kimberly shyly. "My name is Bethany. Want to play? Laura and I already have the doll babies." She pointed to her friend in the corner, a little tow-headed girl in pigtails and overalls.

Ross smiled in relief, but to his disappointment Kimberly wouldn't budge. "No, thank you. I'm staying with my daddy. Let's go home now, Daddy." She tugged on Ross's hand. "Please."

Ross stared at her reluctantly, unsure what to do. This, he hadn't counted on. Had he gone to all the trouble to place Kimberly in a school for nothing?

Linda was back. Having witnessed the last exchange, she touched his shoulder. When he looked into her eyes, he knew she still thought it was past time he moved on and left his daughter in her capable care.

"Better get a move on, Ross, or you're going to be late," she said gently. Then to Kimberly, she said, "You know what? I'm so glad you're here today! It's going to be a really fun morning. We've got finger painting. And we're going to read stories and sing songs. Later we'll have cookies and juice." She smiled. "Doesn't that sound like fun? I bet you like to finger paint. I bet you can really make a neat picture."

"Well..." Kimberly looked tempted for the first time that morning. "If Daddy stays, I will."

It was all Ross could do not to groan. He bent down on his knee, fully intending to reassure Kimberly again, let her know she would be fine, even if he wouldn't be there with her. But the look of utter need in those big green eyes, the sudden trembling of her lower lip, canceled out his resolve. He couldn't, wouldn't leave her. "Of course I'll stay if you need me to, honey." Standing again, he said to Linda, "I have to call the bank, let them know I'll be late."

"You're making a mistake," Linda murmured so that only he could hear.

"Mine to make," Ross said back, just as softly.

Meanwhile, Kimberly continued to hold tightly to his hand. "I'll go with you while you call the bank,

Daddy." Her body had relaxed slightly as she realized he was indeed staying with her. "I don't mind."

When they returned to Linda's classroom, six other children had arrived. All said goodbye to their parents without a qualm, which made Ross feel even worse.

However he'd made the decision to stay with her, and he would do so cheerfully. As he'd hoped, as more time passed, Kimberly began to relax. By nine-thirty, she had left his side long enough to choose her own toys from the shelves.

Linda used the opportunity to pull Ross aside. "Isn't there something you can do to put her at ease?" she whispered.

"Afraid not, not the way she's feeling," he whispered back, a smile fixed on his face.

"But—"

Determined the children wouldn't hear any of this exchange, Ross nudged Linda into a corner. "Trust me on this, would you? I know what I'm doing. And right now my daughter needs me. Okay?"

"But—" Clearly, she still felt he was wrong. Other people didn't do this when they took their kids to school.

Still she held her breath as Kimberly returned and grabbed onto his leg. "Hi, Daddy. I'm back," Kimberly announced cheerfully, the underlying message being her father had better not leave.

Ignoring Ross, Linda bent down and spoke gently to Kimberly, complimenting her on how pretty she looked in her new dress. That said, she then moved off to organize the first major activity of the day. While Linda worked, Kimberly talked briefly to two other children. Later, she participated in the finger painting and the chatter.

Ross stayed a little longer, and finally his diligence paid off. When the class went outside for morning recess, Kimberly left his side long enough to go climb on the monkey bars with the rest of the kids. Nonetheless, she kept checking every minute or so to ensure her father hadn't left.

Observing his dismay, Linda moved to stand beside him, still keeping an eye on the kids. "I hope you know what you're doing," she said softly, her strong disapproval of his indulgence showing once again.

"I do," Ross promised. "She will adjust. It's just going to take her a little time."

"And in the meantime?" Linda whispered back. "What do you do? Go to school with her every day?" Her voice was droll, but there was disappointment there too, the accusation he'd inadvertently let his daughter down in some fundamental way, by not preparing her well enough for this eventuality and by giving in to her petulant demands he stay on.

He looked at Linda, his determination evident. "Until she can relax enough to be here by herself, yes, I think I should come to school with her. Even if it means I have to take some vacation from the bank."

She visually checked on all the children, then sent him another brief but dissenting glance. He was straying into her territory now, and stepping on her toes.

"I think Kimberly will adjust to being here sooner if you'd just give her a chance to grow, to strike out on her own—even if it's temporarily painful for you both."

The fact that Linda thought he was smothering Kimberly, that his daughter was taking advantage of him, stung. "I'm not one of those people who thinks you can teach a child to swim by just throwing her in the river," he countered grimly. For the children's sake, he tried his best to look as if they were chatting amiably.

"That's not what I'm saying and you know it." Her chin high, her smile welcoming, Linda strode off to rescue a four-year-old whose shoelace had come untied.

Ross thought about following her and surreptitiously continuing their argument, then dismissed the idea. What was important here was Kimberly and her feelings, her need for security. What Linda thought of him didn't matter in the least.

The rest of the morning continued pleasantly enough. Pretending not to notice Linda's veiled disapproval, Ross took off his coat and tie, and rolled up his shirt sleeves. He helped with the work sheets for an alphabet game, and later with the color-cut-and-paste project. Without either of them realizing it, Kimberly finally blended in with the rest of the class. As they were cleaning up, she walked over to her father and tapped him impatiently on the leg. "It's okay, now, Daddy. You can go." She sounded almost anxious to be rid of him.

He smiled. This was precisely what he had been hoping for. "You're sure?" He knelt down to be eye level with her.

Kimberly nodded solemnly. "I'll be okay. I'll see you tonight, okay?" She hugged him tightly around the neck, for a second betraying her own lingering unease, and then withdrew. She lifted her chin, showing him her determination to go it alone now. To be grown up. Ross felt tears fill his eyes. Damn, but he loved her.

Watching the emotional exchange between father and daughter, Linda felt a welter of emotions. She was glad Kimberly had finally taken a giant step toward independence—it was much needed. And although she disagreed with Ross on his indulgent handling of his daughter, she felt children needed to know their limits, that it ultimately increased their security, rather than decreased it; she was also glad to see his prediction had been right, that Kimberly would relax, given time and his continuing presence.

Certainly she could see his genuine love for his daughter, and hers for him. It was there in every visual exchange, every word, every hug.

What would it be like to have a child, her own child, love her that way? Linda wondered, experiencing a faint wave of longing.

Resolutely she shrugged off the unexpected sentimentality. And the reluctant envy she felt for every adult who shared the love of a child. In this respect, she knew how both her brothers felt. They had all hoped to have families of their own by now, and the fact that no one but the reckless, irreverent Mike had managed it had surprised them all.

But her time would come, she told herself firmly.

"Well, I'm going." Ross said, interrupting her reverie. He held his coat jacket over one arm. He looked happy and at ease again.

Linda smiled, all too aware that for a while there he'd seriously considered her wisdom as a teacher, and she his as a parent. "I'm glad she's settled down," she said softly, nodding at Kimberly.

"So am I. I feel a lot better now about leaving her. If I'd gone any earlier, well, I would have just worried."

And worried some more, Linda thought. If there was one thing she knew now it was that Ross worried in abundance. But maybe that, too, would be fixed with time. "Well, now you can both relax."

Ross's mouth crooked up wryly. "Yeah, I know." He gave her a steady look that communicated his attraction to her and his silent thanks for not making a scene earlier. "Well... I'll see you later."

Linda nodded, watching as he took his leave, wondering if she could stand waiting to see him again. She had to smile at the feeling, a remnant of her old dependency needs.

TO LINDA'S RELIEF, the rest of the week flew by without a problem. Kimberly said goodbye to her father every day, without the tearful petulance of her first day at school. Linda was gladdened and took heart. Kimberly's tendency to be dependent kept her wary, however.

She saw Ross in passing now and then, but most of the time both were too busy to talk. And in a way, for Linda, that was as much a relief as it was an inconvenience. She didn't want to get too involved with him, under the circumstances.

Despite their successful beginning, though, when Friday afternoon came she was glad the week was over. So was Glenna.

"I can't believe I'm getting married tonight," she said at two o'clock, as she prepared to leave for her appointment at the hairdresser's.

Linda hadn't wanted her to come in to work at all that day, but Glenna had insisted, saying if she stayed home she would only worry and get nervous. Hence, she had allowed herself just enough time to relax for a bit, prepare, and get to the church on time.

"I can't believe you're getting married tonight, either," Linda said. The past month had literally flown by for all of them.

"You're coming aren't you?" For a second, Glenna betrayed her pre-wedding nerves.

"I'll be at the church at seven-thirty," Linda promised, giving her coworker a reassuring hug. "Now scoot! I'll see you later."

Thankfully, the rest of the afternoon went without incident. Linda said a personal goodbye to each student as his or her parent came. Last to arrive was Tad's mother, Wendy.

Linda knew Wendy wanted to talk to her about something—she had said as much on the phone when she called earlier.

While Tad busied himself drawing a picture with magic markers, Linda and Wendy retired to an opposite corner of the classroom. "I have some bad news," Wendy began candidly. "Rob, my ex-husband, hasn't come through with the support payment yet, and frankly, I wouldn't count on him ever coming through. The way things stand, there's no way I can pay next month's tuition or even my utilities. I've barely got enough to cover my rent and enough groceries to tide us over." Her face was white, with splotches of red in her cheeks. "If you could just wait a month or two, I promise you I'm good for the tuition. I'll pay you back one hundred percent even if I have to take out a loan."

Linda hesitated. She knew Ross would disapprove of this from a business standpoint, but from a personal one, she didn't see how she could turn Wendy down. And she was a person who let her feelings guide her. "It's all right," Linda reassured her. Having been through a divorce two years ago herself, she knew how tough the adjustment period could be, and she'd been one of the lucky ones. She'd had few financial worries, no children and a responsible ex-husband. Wendy had practically everything going against her—little money, no other family to fall back on, and last but not least, a musician ex-husband who was both irresponsible and often unemployed. She loved her son very much; in fact, Tad was her whole world.

Currently, they were living in an efficiency apartment above a garage, and Wendy was driving a car that was about to fall apart. Her only extravagance, if one could call it that, was Tad's school. Although she could have opted for cheaper, less quality-oriented day-care, Wendy wanted the best for her son while she was at work and real-estate school.

"How are you otherwise?" Linda asked.

Wendy shrugged, looking tired. "Okay. Coping. Well," she amended softly, "maybe not, but I'm getting there day by day."

"How are your classes going?"

"Okay. They're hard. I've had to study an awful lot." She sent an apologetic look to her son. "But Tad seems to understand. Anyway, it's a terrific opportunity for me to better myself."

"Then go for it," Linda encouraged with a smile.

Tad had begun to gather up his things, and Wendy prepared to go, but hesitated once again on the way out, a grateful look on her face. "I meant what I said about paying you, Linda. I will, I promise, just as soon as I can."

"I know you will." Unlike her ex, Wendy had never been anything but reliable.

After they'd left, Linda finished cleaning up, then locked up and went home. Briefly she considered calling Ross and telling him about the extension she had granted Wendy, then decided against it. She trusted that Wendy would come through with the tuition in a couple of weeks. She would talk to Ross about it then.

In the meantime there was no rush. And she had a wedding to attend.

"LOVELY WEDDING, wasn't it?" Ross said several hours later.

If he was still upset with her over her attitude toward Kimberly's clingy defiance the first day of school, he wasn't showing it, Linda noted, relieved. She knew he was too close to the situation to appreciate her point of view, and she could only hope that one day he would realize it wasn't always in his best interest or his daughter's for him to be guided strictly by emotion. Because where children were concerned, the ability to think coolly and rationally, to act in a thoughtful, consistent manner, was just as important as acting kindly.

Realizing Ross was still waiting for an answer, Linda nodded in agreement. "I thought the ceremony was wonderful, too. Glenna looked lovely, Martin handsome and composed."

"And they managed to recite their vows without giggling or stuttering," Ross added as he stopped a passing waiter and got them each a glass of champagne. She accepted the glass he handed her with thanks, wondering if it was a symbolic peace offering. His eyes met hers and he continued smoothly, "It's not an easy thing to manage when you're nervous."

Linda knew. Because she was nervous now. Something about Ross always put her on edge. Made her feel almost young again, full of youthful yearning.

"Nervous? Who? Me?" Overhearing Ross's remark by chance, a glowing Glenna waltzed over to join them.

"Not us," Martin said, grinning. "We're just ecstatic."

Glenna turned around and waved at the members of the jazz combo hired to play for the occasion. Suddenly she said to Linda and Ross, "Hey, you two look nice together."

At that, it was all Linda could do not to blush.

Was it her imagination or did Ross also blush at Glenna's obvious try at matchmaking?

"Isn't the band terrific?" Glenna continued. Still bubbling over with excitement, she turned back to Ross and Linda. "Have you been dancing?"

"Uh, no. Not yet," Linda said, paling slightly as she contemplated what might be coming next.

"Ross?" Glenna probed animatedly.

"No, I, uh, was busy at the buffet," he said as the soft strains of a wildly romantic ballad began in the background.

Glenna let out a huff of dismay. "You and everyone else in the place! I swear! No one here is enjoying this band! And after all the trouble we went to hire them!" She cast a glance at the empty dance floor, then turned back to them emphatically. "Well, the both of you have got to dance! Don't they, Martin?"

It was all Linda could do to stifle a groan. Never before had Glenna displayed such leadership ability. It was just Linda's luck that her friend, and employee, would pick now to get bossy.

Martin shrugged, studying the other guests, most of whom were seated and not mingling. "It probably would help get things started."

Linda knew what they meant. So far, despite the best efforts of the band, few people were dancing. Oh, Martin and Glenna had taken a spin or two around, but very few others had ventured out. As hosts of the reception, they feared that everyone would not have a perfect time.

"Look, I—" Linda began, planning to beg off. But before she could get to her powder-room excuse, the bride had interrupted her again.

"Martin's right. What we need here is a few guests to break the ice." She smiled winningly at Ross, relying on him to come to her rescue.

To Linda's surprise, Ross seemed to glow. "Shall we, Linda?" he said rising.

"I guess so," she said, taking his outstretched hand.

She slid into his embrace easily, too easily, and began to follow his steps.

"Well, they look happy," Ross said eventually, smiling at the newlyweds.

Before she could help herself, the next words came tumbling out. "Most people do look happy on their wedding day," Linda returned, with an excess of irony.

His brows lifted in response.

Realizing she'd gone overboard in addressing him so tersely, she flushed. She wasn't sure why weddings made her feel irascible.

Ross gave her a sharp, questioning look. "Is that an observation born of experience?" he asked in an amused but tolerant voice, his eyes creasing slightly at the outside corners. "Or just your personal opinion?"

Again, it was all Linda could do not to groan out loud. She'd taken great pains to put up an emotional wall between them. Now he was tearing it down without so much as a bat of an eye.

"It's a little of both, I guess." Linda looked away, trying not to enjoy the press of his chest against her.

But Ross's curiosity was still piqued.

"Weddings are hard for you, aren't they?" he observed quietly, not about to let up now that he'd discovered something about her.

Linda sighed, realizing she had little to gain by hiding her feelings from him. He'd draw his own conclusions. "After my divorce, all weddings were difficult for me at first," she said. "Mainly because I hate to fail at anything, and I failed at my marriage. But it wasn't as hard as it might've been. The split was amicable."

"Still it must have hurt, ending your marriage," he said.

"Yes, I suppose so—or at least it comes out at odd moments, like now." She appreciated his sensitivity to her and decided to do her own probing. "You enjoy weddings, don't you?" she asked, taking in his exquisitely tailored navy jacket, the starched light blue shirt, and coordinating Paisley tie. As always, he was elegantly dressed, whereas she, unaccustomed to high heels, was aware of an ache in both her arches.

Ross glanced at Glenna and Martin. They were posing for pictures in front of the cake. "Yes, I guess I do enjoy weddings, maybe because they always seem to generate so many happy memories for me. Like now." He nodded at Glenna and Martin, who were still posing, the knife poised over the cake. "I think Karen and I spent the whole reception posing for pictures, too."

Linda could imagine the happiness he'd felt, and she envied his sentimental streak. "You miss your wife, don't you?" she asked softly, without thinking.

He nodded. "Yes, I do. Especially at times like now." He spoke matter-of-factly, with no lingering grief, as if he'd accepted a long time ago the hand fate had dealt him. He smiled. "But I have Kimberly, and for that I'm very thankful."

Linda noted how his face changed, became guarded. He knew she disapproved of his indulgence of Kimberly. She suspected that at some point father and daughter would experience a crisis and hoped Ross had the wisdom to deal with it when it came. For now, she could only linger in his arms and savor the new emotions coursing through her because of this man. Emotions she couldn't let see the light of day without compromising her professional scruples.

ON SATURDAY EVENING, all was quiet. Kimberly, exhausted from her first week at school, was already upstairs asleep. Mrs. Delancey was in her room watching television and knitting. Ross was sitting at the kitchen table, attempting to begin his review of the preschool's finances. But so far, all he could think about was the night before, and how Linda Harrigan had looked in that dark blue silk dress. The long sleeves had hugged her slender arms, the high-necked bodice had outlined her womanly curves to perfection. The short, straight skirt, navy-hued stockings, and high heels had made the most of her shapely legs. Her hair had hung loose and curly and wild. Her perfume had been hauntingly sexy.

He hadn't expected his reaction. And even if he had, there was no way he could have been braced for the way her classy, feminine appearance socked him in the middle. He didn't want to think of Linda as a woman, dammit. He wanted to think of her as an educator and business partner—period. He'd been having trouble before, but now he knew he would never see her again without remembering, and without fighting, his own reaction. The reaction of a man to a woman he desired on a very primal level. When combined with his lingering annoyance over her attitude toward his protectiveness of Kimberly, the end result had been confusion and intrigue, and more mixed emotions.

He knew, of course, that Linda didn't really understand his protectiveness of his daughter, but then, he really couldn't expect her to understand because she wasn't a parent. And until you were actually a parent, you just couldn't know how deep those parent-child feelings ran. Or how strong.

So he forgave Linda that.

Trying to forget how she felt in his arms, how enchanting she looked, was another matter. Particularly when he noticed a problem in the books.

For an hour now, he'd been going over the Center's ledger, and trying to quell the knot forming in his stomach.

It had been a banner first week in many ways, and in other ways it had not. Currently, there were twenty-three children enrolled in the Harrigan-Hollister Enrichment Center. There were three paid teachers on the staff, including Linda. They needed at least thirty-six regular students to break even, forty to turn a small profit. To make the Center worthwhile from a financial standpoint, they needed to expand to six classrooms, and approximately seventy-two students. He and Linda had decided to build and then limit enrollment to twelve children in each class, feeling that was all a preschool teacher could reasonably handle.

Linda kept assuring him they would get there, given time. In his head he knew that was true. Yet he continued to worry. He feared he was gambling away the insurance money he'd inherited after Karen's death.

True, he'd set it up financially so he couldn't lose much over the short term, maybe a couple of thousand, if that. But if, for instance, the school continued to operate in the red, as it now was, then he'd be putting his and Kimberly's future in jeopardy. If enrollment didn't pick up, say at the end of another year or two, he would have to consider opting out, letting

Linda find another partner. Of course by that time she would have been in operation long enough to get a loan from the bank. And it was probable that, he continued to reassure himself, a loan wouldn't even be necessary. So far, Linda was doing a great job. The school was a pleasant, cheerful, safe, fun place for a child to be. It was in an excellent location, convenient to major highways and the well-to-do northwest Austin suburbs. Currently, people on waiting lists at the good existing preschools had to wait several years. The vacancies at the Center would spread by word of mouth. Enrollment would pick up. He only needed to have patience.

Relaxing slightly, Ross turned his attention to the books again. It was Linda's policy to collect the tuition for the following week on Friday. She'd made a deposit at the bank. He frowned. It wasn't consistent with the figure he'd expected—and was one fee short. He leafed through the pages again. Next to Tad's name was a question mark penciled in red, and the words *will be late*. What the hell? he wondered. Why hadn't Linda said anything about this to him?

"YOU DID WHAT?" Ross repeated incredulously.

Linda had known from the moment Ross showed up Saturday evening, the account books under his arm, that this was going to be a tough encounter, business-wise and personally. Her cheeks flushed, she ushered him into her kitchen, where she'd been writing lesson plans for the following week. "I told Wendy it was all right, that she could be late for a couple of weeks," she repeated calmly. She moved a stack of papers, clearing a place, and gestured for him to take a seat at the table. "Would you like some coffee?"

"No, thanks." He stubbornly refused to sit down. "Why did you do that?" He looked at her like she had a screw loose.

With a great deal more composure than she felt, Linda went to the sink and rinsed out her cup. She poured more coffee and stirred in cream. Then she leaned against the counter and said, "Tad has been one of my students since I opened my home-run program last summer. Wendy's having a rough time of it personally—"

He cut her off gruffly. "We're not running a charity program, Linda."

She bristled. "I know that!" Since when had he become so almighty?

Hands on hips, he stared down at her. "Our business is losing money as it is. We don't have any money to give away!"

He was acting as if this small sum would break them, which was ludicrous. "We have plenty of money in the bank," she countered, her tone stormy.

"Yes, mine, and I'll thank you to consult me first as to how we use it." He scowled at her, the anger he'd felt upon arrival doubled.

Setting her untouched coffee aside, Linda gave him a long, cold look. "Wendy is good for the money."

"Fine. Let her owe someone else then, but we need to be paid. You're setting a precedent here I don't like." He moved restlessly toward her, and then away, prowling the cramped space between counters in the galley-style kitchen.

Crossing one ankle over the other, she held her ground and tried to clear the fury from her head. "I can't say I like the way you're behaving much, either." At that moment, in fact, she disliked just about everything about him. Did he have to be such a nitpicker now, when they'd gotten off to such a good start? Without warning, her frustration welled up and out of control. "Dammit, Ross, you gave me carte blanche to run the Center any way I saw fit!"

He closed the distance between them in two long strides. "And you gave me carte blanche over the business details. This falls under that jurisdiction."

He was close enough to touch. She could smell the faint woodsy scent of his cologne, see the barest stubble of evening beard on his chin. They stood as if engaged for combat, gauging, assessing. She knew that he wouldn't back down and that this was an argument she wouldn't win.

She set her jaw. "Fine, if that's the way you want it, *I'll* pay Tad's tuition." She turned on her heel and whirled in the direction of the hutch. She grabbed her purse off the shelf and extracted her checkbook in one dramatic motion.

For a long moment he said nothing, then in a persuasive tone began, "Linda—"

Too angry to be coaxed into further discussion, she continued writing and snapped, "You want the Center to be paid, the Center will be paid."

He stared at her furiously, every muscle in his body taut, incensed that she wouldn't see matters his way.

When she handed him the check, he refused to take it. His jaw hardened even more. "You're behaving childishly."

"And you're behaving like Scrooge!" She tossed the check in his face and watched as it fluttered, uncaught, to the floor. He looked at her without remorse. She got even angrier. "Don't you have any compassion for others? Where's your sympathy for the less fortunate?" What kind of man was he, anyway?

"I have plenty of compassion for Wendy," he muttered condescendingly, as he kneaded the tension from the back of his neck. "It doesn't mean I can or will support her and her son, or every other needy child who comes around."

She calmed herself slightly and decided to try to win him over with charm. Surely if he knew the whole story he wouldn't be so quick to refuse aid. She smiled warmly. "Wendy and Tad are nice people, Ross. Whether it's good for business or not, I can't just turn my back on them, and I think if you had been the one teaching her son for the past four months, neither would you."

His green eyes narrowed. He wasn't the least bit moved. "Wrong, Linda. I turn down loans to people every day. It's part of business, part of life. Sometimes you have to say no—no matter how much it hurts."

He bent and picked up the check, refusing to acknowledge her plea. When he spoke again, his voice was icy and curt. "If you want to pay Tad's tuition, I can't stop you." He clipped it to the inside of the account book with exaggerated care.

His false display of tolerance grated on her nerves like fingernails on a chalkboard. "But you disapprove?"

He met her gaze equably and said, enunciating clearly, "Yes. I think you're wrong."

She stared at him, wondering what she'd gotten herself into by agreeing to this partnership, and who this man really was.

"You know what I think?" she countered silkily, her anger really churning now. "I think you're afraid to get involved, afraid to feel, afraid to risk. You've isolated yourself, Ross, and you've isolated your daughter. And somewhere, some way, it has to stop."

Chapter Four

Was Linda right about him? Ross wondered. Had he turned into a selfish Scrooge? The question haunted him long after he left her home, her check for Tad's tuition tucked securely into the Center's ledger where it stayed all weekend.

If he were honest, he had to admit he *had* changed since his wife's death. Before that he'd never imagined anything so terrible could happen to him. Oh, he knew people were killed in accidents every day, but not his wife. Not the mother of his child.

At first he'd been numb, and the numbness had continued for days after the funeral. He hadn't really believed this tragedy had happened to him. And then the guilt had set in—he could've prevented Karen's death if only he'd followed his gut instincts and kept her home that night. He'd kept thinking, hoping, that one day he would wake up and find it had all been a bad dream. Only he hadn't woken up. And eventually he'd known it was true, that his wife was dead, and no matter how he loved her she wasn't coming back

Only Kimberly had kept him going. He'd known he had to be strong for her, and he had been. But doing so had cost him; he was just beginning to learn how much. He also knew it was past time for him to start moving forward again, to come out of his protected, self-involved world and join the human race again. And to that end, he knew just where he had to start.

So, taking a chance she wasn't still livid and wouldn't throw him out on sight, he drove to Linda's house Sunday evening. As he'd hoped, she was home and answered the door almost immediately. When she saw who it was, her expression changed from one of welcome to wariness.

He felt a moment's unease. Maybe dropping by unannounced wasn't such a good idea, after all. But if he'd called, she might have refused to see him—or agreed, but been chilly. His resolve would have sagged. Besides, this was something better done in person.

"Is it all right if I come in?" he said.

Linda stared at him from across the threshold, her expression going from wary to inscrutable. Finally she lifted an indifferent shoulder, and then inclined her head in the direction of the family room.

As she led him silently into the center of the house, he looked around. The room that had once housed her class had been returned to a normal state. Two garnet tuxedo sofas graced the white stone fireplace. The shelves were filled with books, knickknacks, a stereo and portable television. Leafy green plants hung from the ceiling. Colorful magazines decorated the bleached-oak end and coffee tables. Paintings—most of them primitive art—hung on the wall.

Still not speaking, Linda picked up the needlepoint she'd been working on and seated herself on one of the sofas. The expression she was embroidering said:

Compliments of the Chef, and featured a smoking pan.

"I'm surprised you're out tonight," she said blandly, as she moved the embroidery needle in and out of the webbed fabric.

He knew by the glint in her eyes she was baiting him. Still he couldn't resist. "Why?" For the moment he remained standing.

"Oh, I don't know." Her voice was wry as she jabbed the needle in and out with daunting swiftness.

From the look of satisfaction on her face, he imagined that she imagined she was poking the needle into his skin. He had to work not to laugh. This haughty, puritanical manner was so unlike her.

She sighed, then said, "I guess I figured you'd be at home counting pennies—or maybe saving bits of twine and string."

Her comment about his stinginess found its target. But strangely enough he wasn't offended, merely amused, because he knew darn well he'd had it coming—even if she was wrong about haphazardly giving out a scholarship without consulting him. In the past, before he'd been hit by bad fortune himself, he hadn't been so parsimonious. Nor did he intend to be so uncharitable in the future.

Deciding a less-formal demeanor was in order, he took an upholstered armchair catercorner to her, all too aware that an episode of *Murder, She Wrote* was still playing on the television and that Linda was making no effort to turn it down.

"Yes, well, I want to apologize for yesterday," he began.

She lifted her head to meet his eyes directly, as she realized his peacemaking efforts were genuine. "Does that mean you think you were wrong?"

He edged forward slightly in his chair, sensing her continuing disapproval but not disturbed by it. "In principle? No. I think I was right. It was irresponsible of you to make a decision like that without consulting me first." About that, he was firm.

Her scowl deepened and she dropped her gaze to her needlework. "Then why are you here?"

He waited until she looked up again before he answered. "Because I know your heart was in the right place."

His words were greeted with utter silence. He found her persistent coolness wearing thin. He could think of only one way to end it, and that was by explaining his actions—something else he was unaccustomed to doing. Nonetheless, he thought grimly, this was one time it had to be done—for the sake of their mutual business, for the sake of their fledgling friendship.

Suddenly restless, he got up to pace the room. "What you said about me shutting myself off struck a chord." He paused at the sliding-glass doors to the patio and backyard, now filled with late-day dusky gray light. He turned back to Linda and continued in a voice that was anything but proud, "I realized you were right."

His apology opened the door to mutual understanding. Linda reached forward and picked up the TV remote control. She turned the set off, put aside her needlepoint, and waited for him to go on.

Aware he had her full attention now, he said, "My wife was killed in a traffic accident."

Linda looked shocked, but by the set of her jaw, he could see that she'd decided to let him go on without interruption or murmurs of sympathy.

"The days and months that followed were very difficult. It was all I could do to carry on. Kimberly was only two. She missed her mother desperately, and she wasn't old enough to understand death, the finality of it. There was no way I could explain it. She just felt deserted and confused." His eyes misted and he felt the familiar tightening in his gut. "There were plenty of nights where I just held her while she cried for her mommy. It was a difficult time." In fact, if there was such a thing as hell on earth, that had been it for him.

Without warning, she left the sofa to stand beside him. Not touching, but just letting him know she was there to listen. "I'm sorry, Ross."

He nodded, accepting her sympathy, then turned to face her squarely. Before he realized what he was doing, he found himself uncharacteristically asking for her forgiveness. "I never meant to isolate Kimberly or myself, it just evolved that way, I guess." He swallowed hard. "Between my work and trying to give Kimberly enough time and attention, there wasn't room for anything or anyone else." Linda seemed to understand, and he found himself continuing way past the point he had initially planned. His voice calm but weary, he confided, "Last night, when you called me Scrooge, I realized maybe that was what I had become." He shook his head, reflecting. "I didn't like the image very much."

She touched his forearm lightly, in the way a friend comforts a friend. "I didn't mean to hurt you, Ross."

But she had. And she'd also woken him up. He nodded and she dropped her arm. "But you had a valid point," he went on determinedly. "And it got me to thinking—not just about what we argued about, but the situation in general." His voice took on an undertone of excitement as he got to what he'd really come to talk about. Something he knew she'd relate to and approve of. "Maybe... maybe there is something we can do, and not just for Tad, but for other kids of limited means who are in need of quality preschool or day-care."

Linda looked at him questioningly. "What do you mean?"

"I think we need to look for a way to provide scholarships to needy students. We can do it through private benefactors or maybe one of the civic-minded organizations like the Junior Forum."

Her features softened as she realized he'd not only done an about-face but was serious about fixing the situation so it never came up again. They could still meet their obligations, yet act from their hearts, too.

Linda moved away to sit back down on the sofa, but didn't resume her needlepoint. "You weren't the only person who was in the wrong yesterday, Ross." Sensing his approval, she continued solemnly. "I've been thinking a lot this afternoon, too. You were right about what you said last night. First and foremost, we are running a business. Sometimes, in my zeal to try to help the children I lose sight of that."

And they both knew that if they couldn't turn a profit they'd never be able to stay in business. Sooner or later the school would be forced to close, and then they'd all lose.

Feeling more relaxed than he had in a long time, Ross moved to sit opposite her. He sensed she had more to say, so he waited patiently.

"We might get our enrollment up quickly by approaching corporate sponsors and seeing if they'll subsidize the care of their employees' children at the Center."

"Which in turn would encourage the employees to place their children in our school." Ross paused briefly, mulling over the way those words had sounded. Our school.

He brought his attention back to her. "Do you have any specific company in mind?"

She nodded, her own attitude as businesslike as his. For the next thirty minutes they discussed this latest idea, formed to salvage the school and their relationship, and studied the list of companies Linda had put together.

"Hmm," Ross said when at last they decided to give themselves a break. He knew he should leave, yet something in him bade him to linger just a little longer. "Considering what ideas we reaped from our argument yesterday, it wasn't all for naught."

She grinned, then looked at him directly, a new humility in her eyes. The moment lengthened pleasurably before she said softly, "We do need to work together more closely, Ross." She paused. "I'm willing to try, if you are."

He smiled, realizing he hadn't been wrong about her, after all. She was a born businesswoman, as well as a teacher, destined to be successful. They both were. And once they worked out the kinks in this new partnership of theirs, they'd make a very good team indeed.

"THAT'S IT! I QUIT!" Glenna stormed at Linda as she entered Linda's office early Monday morning two weeks later. Because there were only two of them there so far, she felt free to plop into a chair next to the door.

"Not your job, I hope?" Linda said, aghast. She didn't know what she would do without Glenna.

"No, my marriage. I have to face it. It's been just a little over two weeks and already the honeymoon is over! He won't take out the trash except once a week, and he yells at me for leaving the cap off the toothpaste. I'm telling you, Linda. Martin is turning into a damned poor roommate. And frankly, I just don't know if I can take it."

Linda remembered the disillusionment she'd felt when her marriage had gradually foundered. Sometimes she thought she'd expected too much all along, and so had been primed for disappointment. At other times, she felt she'd not demanded enough of Gene and that if she had pushed it might've worked out—or ended in a blaze of passion, instead of just fading slowly away into nothing. Nonetheless, it was far too soon for Glenna to give up trying.

Linda shook her head ruefully, then let Glenna have it with both guns. "Where is it written you have to divide the tasks sexistly? If it bothers you, then you take the garbage out. And as for the toothpaste, buy two tubes."

Glenna gave her a droll look. "You've got a point about the toothpaste. But as for the other, it's not just the garbage that's the issue. Martin is turning out to be woefully lacking in anything domestic."

Unlike Ross, Linda thought, who'd proved himself to be a pro in the kitchen on Saturday night at her house, when they'd entertained several possible corporate clients.

"That's what you get for marrying an engineer, Glenna," Ross commented, entering just in time to hear the last part of Glenna's complaint. He stood in the doorway, filling it as usual with his handsome frame. He'd just dropped off Kimberly and had come looking for Linda before heading off to work. "Engineers love to take things apart and put them back together again, but that's about all."

Glenna shook her head, deliberately tamping down her amusement at Ross's gentle teasing. "You're a lot of help, Ross."

He beamed. "Anytime."

"Which reminds me," Glenna said, getting up. "About the Thanksgiving pageant—"

"What pageant?" Ross interrupted.

"The one we're planning to have every year," Linda said.

"Oh. Have you found a place for it yet?"

"Well, as a matter of fact, I have. The McNeil elementary school has agreed to let me use both their stage and their cafeteria facilities the Wednesday evening before Thanksgiving. We'll have to build our own scenery, though."

"I'd like to be in charge of writing the dialogue for the play," Glenna said.

"That'd be great."

"Can I help?" Ross asked Linda.

She hedged. She knew how driven he could be when he got going on something. More bossing from him she didn't need. Unfortunately, since it was already early October, there was no way she could manage to get everything done that needed to be done unless she accepted his help. And anyone else's who was interested in lending a hand. "Sure," she said, forcing a smile.

"Just tell me what, when and where—" Ross was interrupted by a loud shriek and the pounding of feet. "What in the world...?"

He and Linda charged out of the office just in time to see Dexter running down the hall, a water gun in his hand. Oblivious to the adults behind them, Kimberly dashed full speed into Linda's classroom, Dexter hot on her heels. By the time Linda and Ross caught up with them, Kimberly was jumping from a child-sized chair to the tabletop. Dexter was leaping up to follow. Squeezing the trigger twice, he aimed a spray of water at Kimberly's face, eliciting yet another screech from her.

"All right, you two. Hold it right there," Linda intervened sternly.

Kimberly and Dexter turned guiltily.

She held out her hand. "Dexter, the gun, please."

Reluctantly he surrendered the water-filled plastic weapon. "Where did you get this, Dexter?"

"It belongs to my big brother. He said I could play with it if I didn't bother him while he talked to Cindy on the phone."

"I see." Somehow this didn't surprise Linda. From what she knew of Dexter's five older brothers and sisters and the no-limits environment his scholarly parents fostered, he lived in a home that was sometimes like a college fraternity house. Because of the constant unconscious tutoring he was receiving from older siblings, he was very precocious. All of which was very new and thrilling to Kimberly, an only child.

Looking perturbed by the whole incident, Ross walked forward and used a cloth handkerchief to blot the excess moisture from his daughter's hair. Kimberly moved away slightly, as if resenting his babying her in front of a peer.

"What's our rule about running, either inside or outside the school?" Linda asked the children.

"We don't do it," Kimberly said.

"Why not?"

"Because we might trip and hurt ourselves," Dexter said.

"We also have a rule about not bringing toys from home, don't we?"

Dexter nodded and ducked his head in shame.

"I'm going to keep your water gun, Dexter, until you go home today. Then I'll give it back. But if you bring it to school again, I will not give it back. Do you understand?"

He nodded.

"And Kimberly, no more screaming. If you have a problem, please tell a teacher, okay?"

"Okay." She, too, continued looking at the floor.

Just then, the new staff teacher, Helen Masterson, a vivacious middle-aged woman with a particularly soothing presence appeared in the doorway. Getting the signal visually from Linda that she was through scolding the children, Helen said, "I need some helpers to sort crayons for me! Kimberly, Dexter, want to come?"

Both children looked at Linda, who nodded. "I'll keep an eye on everyone until classes start at nine," Helen promised.

The three walked off. Linda saw Tad coming in, too, minus his mother, and realized Wendy had probably just dropped him off.

"Can I talk to you for a minute?" Ross said.

Linda didn't like the thunder she heard in his voice, but nodded anyway. "In my office."

As soon as she shut the door, ensuring them privacy, Ross asked, "Does Dexter do this kind of thing often?"

"What kind of thing?" she asked, feigning ignorance.

"Behave in a disruptive, potentially dangerous manner."

"Ross—"

"Suppose that had been a real gun he'd brought to school. Something he picked up at home. Suppose he had accidentally tripped or fallen and really hurt himself or Kimberly while chasing around the school. What then?"

"First of all, he wouldn't bring a real gun. Even if his parents have one, which I doubt, they're too smart to leave it lying around. Second, if Dexter or Kimberly had gotten hurt, we would have dealt with it. But I think I'm right in guessing that it isn't really Dexter you're worried about, it's Kimberly. You just didn't like her being chased."

"Can you blame me?"

Dexter was often rowdy and disruptive, and it wasn't anything to get upset about. Ignoring Ross's question, Linda tried to reason with him. "Look, Ross, it takes all kinds of people to make this world go round. And that's what preschool is all about. Learning to deal with the different personalities."

"Is Dexter like that all the time?" Ross asked. "I mean, I've heard stories from Kimberly. She says he's always getting into trouble on the playground by trying to go down the slide face first, or pulling some girl's hair."

That was true, Linda knew. But all were relatively minor infractions. Just because Dexter tried to get away with a lot didn't mean he was very successful. In fact, he almost always got caught before the crime; this morning was an exception. She explained all this to Ross, finishing, "The main problem is he just hasn't adjusted to being in a different class yet. I think he will. And I know Glenna is doing her best with him, giving him extra time and attention."

"Well, I still don't like it," Ross said, frowning. "I think by continuing to have Dexter here, we're just asking for trouble."

His willingness to send Dexter away infuriated Linda. "And who will take care of him if we don't?" she said, advancing on him, her hands on her hips. "Children are our first priority here, Ross. Not law and order. Besides, it's the kids like Dexter, the potential clowns and misfits in the world, whom we should reach at this level. I want to show them how to excel and create, yet still fit in, be accepted socially by their peers, before they get to elementary school and get lost in the system, branded a failure or a strange bird for life."

Ross sighed. Linda sensed that if it weren't for Kimberly and her potential safety Ross would've agreed with her. "I still don't like it," he said, his green eyes darkening. "Don't forget, I have a say here, too," he countered when she would have argued.

"Only in the business side," Linda shot back. "Not on who we enroll. There was nothing in our partnership agreement about that!"

"My mistake," he replied acerbically.

Linda stared at him, refusing to back down. Ross saw he wasn't getting anywhere with her. He glanced at his watch. "I've got to go. I'll tell Kimberly goodbye on my way out."

She let him go without another word.

The morning continued smoothly. But try as she might, she couldn't get the morning's incident or Ross's misguided priorities out of her mind. Whether she wanted to admit it or not, they were at odds, and perhaps would always be over a very vital issue. Ross was determined to protect his daughter at any cost, no matter what other child might be hurt in the process. But Linda, as director of the preschool, was looking out for *every* child in the school. She could only hope they wouldn't come to blows over anything else along those lines, because she was genuinely beginning to care for the man, in ways she didn't want to acknowledge.

"YOU'RE STILL PEEVED at me for my views on Dexter, aren't you?" Ross said when he met with Linda later the next evening to begin working on the backdrop for the Thanksgiving pageant. They were in her garage workshop. Glenna and Martin were on their way over. But so far, it was just Ross and Linda putting together the pieces of precut lumber that would represent the *Mayflower* in the planned reenactment of the landing at Plymouth Rock.

Hammering the nails to join the wooden mast with the ship's frame, Linda said, "I'm not mad, I'm just disappointed. I think you were overreacting, but then that's normal. A lot of parents do it, especially when their first child is in school."

Ross winced as she delivered the last few hammer blows with strong, sure strokes. "Well, maybe you're right. Maybe. But I still have some reservations."

Linda hadn't really expected Ross to be so reasonable. Amazed, she stopped what she was doing and looked up at him. "You know, maybe it would help if you got to know Dexter a little better. He really is a neat kid. A bit, uh, energetic, but lively and full of ideas."

"Maybe." Ross frowned. He picked up another mast.

"I know when you could do it, too," Linda continued.

"When?"

"During Oktoberfest. We're taking the kids on a field trip to New Braunfels to see the festival, and experience German culture firsthand. You could go, you know. Act as one of the chaperons. We need as many as we can get. We could also use your station wagon, since we're having parents drive in a convoy."

Ross nodded. "Okay, I'll go. But I'm not promising to take a miraculous liking to this kid. If he is as sweet as you say, then we'll probably hit it off. But if not..."

Linda grinned, feeling she'd already won this skirmish. "Don't borrow trouble, Ross," she said as a car pulled up at the curb and Glenna and Martin got out and walked toward the garage.

"Just take each day one step at a time." That was what she intended to do.

Chapter Five

"Dexter, please be careful with that spaghetti," Glenna cautioned gently the next day at noon as she handed him his tray. "We don't want it all over your clothes today, okay? Because that Garfield sweatshirt you're wearing is so cute."

Dexter beamed at the compliment. "I'll be careful, I promise," he said shyly.

Linda smiled, glad to see that Glenna and Dexter were getting on better now that he was in her class fulltime. Her thoughts were interrupted by Kimberly.

"Do you like spaghetti?" the little girl asked.

"Yes, I do. Very much. And don't forget to eat your applesauce and breadsticks, everyone," Linda advised cheerfully.

"We won't," said Bethany.

Laura held up an empty fruit dish. "See, I already ate mine!"

"That's very good, Laura," Linda said. Almost finished with her meal, she looked around at her class. Most would need at least fifteen minutes more at the table, which was fine. The kids needed a good long break at midpoint of every school day.

She turned slightly and looked around the room. Helen's class was always the first to enter the lunchroom. Consequently they were all seated at a table ahead of Linda. Glenna's class was to the rear. Each teacher ate with her own class, keeping an eye on them, to ensure everything ran smoothly. Today, however, that was not to be. Linda noticed Tad turning around to stare scornfully at Dexter. Elbowing the little boy next to him, Tad pointed to Dexter's shirt. Despite his best efforts to be neat, spaghetti sauce had dripped down onto Dexter's chin and onto Garfield's eyes.

"Look at that," Tad crowed unkindly. "Garfield's face is all messy, just like Dexter's!"

Dexter looked guiltily down at his shirt and then up at Tad, his expression a symphony of hurt.

Glenna, deep in conversation with two other children in her class, glanced over and frowned at the same time as Linda. Linda gave her signal that indicated she would handle it, then got up to walk to the adjacent tables where the two boys were sitting.

"Tad? May I have a word with you?"

Taking in her stern expression, Tad became immediately defensive. "I didn't do anything," he said, pointing at Dexter. "He's the big baby."

"That's enough, Tad," Linda said firmly. "My office. Now."

Glenna got up and went to comfort Dexter, who was crying. "I'll watch your class, Linda."

"Thanks."

Tad marched on ahead of her, his every clomping step an extension of his tantrum. Linda shut the door behind them as he plopped down into his seat. "What?" he asked belligerently.

That's what Linda wanted to know. In the past two weeks, Tad had gone from a little angel to a disruptive child. "I've never known you to be mean before, Tad. You really hurt Dexter's feelings in there, making fun of him that way. And I know you know better than to behave that way. So what's up? Did you and Dexter have a fight?"

"No," Tad said, his own eyes beginning to fill with tears.

"Then what is it?"

Tad kicked the floor with the toe of his shoe. "I just don't like him anymore, that's all. He's a big baby."

"You used to play together just fine when we only had one class at the Center. In fact, you and Dexter were great buddies."

Silence.

"Did Dexter say something to you?"

"No."

"Did he hit you?"

"No."

"Did he do anything to deserve the mean things you said to him in the lunchroom?"

Silence.

"I think you owe Dexter an apology," Linda said.

More silence. Tad wiped defiantly at his tears. "Do I get to go out with the other kids at recess?"

She hesitated. They had no clear-cut rule about that. It was a judgment call by the teacher, depending on the nature of the infraction, the mood of the disobedient student. She sensed Tad had a lot of pent-up anger and resentment to work out—and the playground seemed the safest outlet. "We'll have to see," she said finally. "Mainly it depends on how you behave yourself during the rest of lunch."

Tad nodded. He went back to the lunchroom and apologized to Dexter, who still looked angry and upset.

Again Linda wondered if there was more going on than she knew. But she had no more time to think about it, for the fifteen-minute playbreak outside had begun, and afterward everyone returned to the classroom for the completion of the day's cooking project. They were going to decorate the gingerbread men they had baked that morning.

The children went about the activity with varying degrees of artistic proficiency. Kimberly was one of the better artists in her group. Linda paused beside her, admiring her smooth application of the decorative white frosting. Beside her, Tad continued to work with unprecedented concentration. Linda guessed he still felt bad about what he'd done to his former best friend, and that this new behavior was positive. She made no effort to draw him out of his introspective mood.

Beside Linda, Kimberly began to chatter, as she always did when she had an adult audience. "Today is my daddy's birthday," she told Linda solemnly, "but he's not going to have a party. He says parties are for kids." Kimberly put two raisins on her gingerbread man for eyes, then looked up at Linda. "Why can't grown-ups have birthday parties?" she asked, her eyes wide.

On either side of Kimberly, working diligently on their gingerbread men, Laura and Bethany chorused, "Yeah, how come?"

"Well, they can," Linda said, surprised by what Kimberly had told her. "If they want parties, that is. But not all adults want to celebrate their birthdays."

"Why not?" Kimberly picked up a yellow M & M and placed it right below the eyes.

"I don't know," Linda said honestly. She watched as Kimberly picked up a small piece of red licorice, which soon became the gingerbread man's mouth. "Some adults don't really like getting older." But that didn't sound like Ross. He didn't come across as a person hung up about age.

So why wouldn't he want a party? Usually he took great pains to see Kimberly got whatever she wanted or needed to make her happy. Yet he was denying his daughter this pleasure. Why?

Curious, she put in a call to Mrs. Delancey. Ross's housekeeper confirmed what Kimberly had told Linda. "Yes, it is his birthday. But he's not letting us do very much about it." She sounded as unhappy as Kimberly about that.

"He's got a cake, surely?" Linda asked. She was the kind of person who liked to get every bit of joy possible out of life. Consequently she couldn't bear the thought of anyone letting a birthday go by uncelebrated.

"Oh, yes, he let me bake his favorite chocolate coconut cake for him. But he said no presents or anything, and frankly, I think that's wrong. Kimberly's already made him a beautiful card, and another picture for his office, which I had framed. But other than that . . ." her voice trailed off, perplexed sounding.

"Is this normal for him?" Linda asked. "Does he usually have a party?"

"Not since I've worked for him," Mrs. Delancey said. In the background, there was a persistent buzz.

"There's my cake. I better get it out of the oven before it burns."

Linda thanked her and hung up.

She was worried about Ross. When they'd formed the partnership he'd been so gung ho. Now, lately, all he seemed to be was worried.

On impulse, she talked to Glenna about it after the children had left for the day. Glenna had much the same reaction as Linda. "Why, that rascal!" Glenna swore good-humoredly. "Ross never said one word about it being his birthday today."

"To me, either," Linda said.

"And he should have a party!"

"I think so, too. But maybe he's not in the mood for one," Linda finished. Although her impulse was to just go ahead and give him one, she feared it might be too forward a thing to do for someone as private as Ross.

"I know what you mean about his being no party animal," Glenna murmured. "He's been about as sociable as a wounded bear all week. I mean, every time he walks in the Center he gets a frown on his face."

Probably because he was mentally calculating the negative cash flow of their business, Linda thought. And the corporate executives and their wives they'd wined and dined the previous weekend had yet to call with an answer to Ross's proposal they act as benefactors or patrons of the school.

Maybe the pressures of working full-time, caring for Kimberly, and co-running a business were getting to him, Linda thought. She hated to think she or the Center were adding to his stress. She sighed, searching her mind for a quick and easy solution. She wanted to land on something that would fix everything somehow.

She cleared her throat. "Personally I think he's been spending too much time at work, and that some rest and recreation is in order."

"I agree." Glenna sighed emphatically. "The only question is how to convince him it is."

At the other teacher's perplexed tone, Linda smiled. She was nothing if not inventive, after all.

Ross had done so much for her. Wasn't it time she did something for him?

"Why don't you leave that to me. Now here's what I've thought up so far..."

"ONE GALLON BLACK PAINT, three gallons brown, two gallons green. Four paintbrushes, wood glue, and sandpaper," Ross said, checking his list and then the items on the cart at the hardware store. He looked at Linda. "Are we forgetting anything?"

"Not that I know of," Linda said, frowning and consulting her own list. The Thanksgiving pageant wasn't far off, and they had a lot of work to do on the scenery. "Oh," she said, "I'm not sure we'll have enough paint for the log cabin. But we can come back later if we need more. We certainly have enough to get started, anyway."

Although Ross had said nothing to her at all about yesterday being his birthday, Linda knew from Kimberly they'd had cake and ice cream the night before at his house. She reported it had been a dull affair, not the exciting party she had wanted.

Again Linda wondered why Ross had resisted, when he gave in to Kimberly on practically everything else. Knowing she still had some time to kill before she took Ross back to her house for the work session on the scenery, she said, "So, how come you don't like birthday parties for yourself?"

"Kimberly told you." He looked amused.

"Yes. So, why don't you?" she prodded, when no explanation was forthcoming.

Ross's mood turned brooding. He answered her question in an indifferent tone. "I guess I just don't think birthdays are that big a deal. For a kid, yes, but not for an adult."

He was hiding something. Linda faked a yawn. "I guess you're right. When you're twenty-one, you're legal for everything."

"Which definitely makes it less exciting," he said, grinning at her rakishly.

Maybe, maybe not, Linda thought. It all depended on who you knew and what you did. For her, she felt the really exciting times of her life were just beginning. But Ross seemed to think that in a lot of respects his life was over now; maybe it was because he was a widower. A shame, she thought, giving up on so much, so soon, widowed or not.

Only when they were on their way back to the car did she speak again. She asked impulsively, "What was your best birthday?"

"The year I was sixteen. I got a car, an old Chevy four-door sedan." He shook his head, remembering. "I really thought I was hot stuff, having wheels of my own."

She could imagine. She'd felt that way about her first car, too. "And your worst birthday?" she asked, as they loaded the supplies into the back of his station wagon.

"My worst was that first year after my wife died." His expression turned sad. "I didn't feel like celebrating much of anything that year." He fell silent.

She had the feeling she was being intrusive. And more, that what he was feeling now wasn't necessarily grief over his loss, but something else just as disturbing and inhibiting. And that had something to do with his wife. Regrets, maybe? Over something he should've said or done, and hadn't? Or something else, something deeper?

In any case, she didn't know him well enough to pursue the line of thought, so she backed off.

Then it became his turn to pursue. Shaking off his somber mood, he asked, "What was your best birthday?" For the briefest second, his eyes probed hers intimately, making her extraordinarily aware of him.

She found herself flushing slightly and ducking her head in unaccustomed shyness as she answered, "My best was the year I turned ten. We were vacationing at Disneyland in California and we celebrated right there in the park. They had a cake for me at one of the restaurants and everything."

Ross grinned. "Neat." He was silent a moment. "And the worst?" he queried softly.

About that, Linda had to think a minute.

Truth be told, she couldn't remember ever really having had a bad birthday. Which just went to show what a lucky life she had led.

"I guess that would've been the first year both my brothers were away from home," she answered finally. "Tom was in college, Mike in the army. It just didn't feel right without them. I called and talked to them long-distance, but I still missed them."

"I know what you mean," he said quietly, smiling. "Family's important."

"Yes, it is." She was glad he understood that. Something else they had in common.

She knew he was anxious to get back to her garage and get to work on the scenery. She didn't try to keep him further. They were both in the door, their arms laden with packages when the lights inside the house flicked on unexpectedly, and a chorus of voices called "Surprise!"

Ross blinked in astonishment at the people who suddenly gathered around him. Helen, Glenna, Martin, Francine and others from the American Heritage Bank where he worked had come to celebrate his birthday. Mrs. Delancey, too. "Daddy, we're having a surprise party just for you!" Kimberly ran forward to greet him. She waved at the streamers hanging from the ceiling. "Isn't it neat? Linda let us get balloons and party hats and everything!"

Ross looked delighted, just as Linda had hoped he'd be. He kissed his daughter and gave her a hug. "It sure is neat." He turned to Linda, a mixture of surprise and wonderment in his eyes, and with that came heartfelt appreciation. "Thank you," he said gently. "Thank you all. This is really something."

Linda grinned. It was the first time she'd ever seen him so happy. Maybe Ross was more of a party animal than he knew. He just needed to be with the right people to bring out that side of him.

Linda was glad she'd been able to help. She felt she was paying him back in some way for all he'd done for her and her school, as if now the mutual kindnesses were balanced more evenly between them.

She wanted to someday get to the point where there were more kindnesses between them than difficulties. And for the first time, she felt that it was happening; that they were business partners, bound together not just by the terms of a legal contract, but by a steadily growing friendship.

"CAN YOU BELIEVE IT? Twenty-four new students in just two weeks!" Linda announced triumphantly to Ross the following afternoon as he seated himself in a chair across from her desk.

Ross stretched out his legs in front of him and loosened his tie. His mouth curved with satisfaction. "Our new sponsor, Lone Star Textbook Publisher, certainly didn't waste any time getting the word out to their employees, once it decided to sponsor us."

She met his eyes and smiled, unable to hide her happiness. She was even starting a new waiting list for openings the next fall.

"I don't have to tell you this latest development really eases my mind," Ross said, appearing as comfortable with her as she was with him. "Especially since we'll be turning a small profit now."

Despite her pleasure, Linda couldn't help but feel disconcerted by his closeness. She could smell the spicy, subtle scent of his after-shave, see a hint of five o'clock shadow on his jaw. With effort she forced herself to concentrate on what he was saying, not how he smelled and looked. They were friends, that was all, right?

"Hiring new teachers should be no problem," she said in as cool, detached a voice as she could muster. "I've got interviews with prospective teachers set up, starting tomorrow." She already had two candidates in mind. Just reading their resumés and having chatted with them briefly on the phone revealed they were everything she wanted.

"You'll let me know how it goes?" he asked, preparing to leave.

Linda nodded. "I promise I'll keep you informed." She paused, watching him.

"I'll be back to help cut out another twenty hats for the pageant."

"Sure, that'll be fine," she responded, smiling. It was great, having Ross so eager to help. Maybe given time, his need to control everything, at least at the Center, might disappear altogether.

"OKAY, SWEETIE, now put the glue all around the cardboard circle. That's it. That's wonderful, Kimberly!" Linda said. "Now we're going to press the black cloth onto the circle—"

"And we have a hat!" Kimberly said.

"Almost." Linda added a black cone to the stiff black brim and stapled them together securely. Kimberly handed her a thick white cloth band Linda had sewn earlier, which gave the finishing touch to the pilgrim's hat. "Want to model this for your daddy?" Linda said.

"Sure!" Grinning from ear to ear, Kimberly stood perfectly still while Linda balanced the hat on her head.

Ross looked up from his paperwork. "Hey, you look great! Nice job, ladies."

"Now we only have to make twenty-four more," Linda said.

Ross groaned, contemplating that task, along with all the business-related paperwork he had. Kimberly, however, was only delighted to be of assistance.

"Can I help?" she said.

"You sure can," Linda said.

"I hate to interrupt," Ross said, watching as his daughter made a half-hearted attempt to smother a gigantic yawn. "But Kimberly, it's past your bedtime. Way past."

Suddenly the little girl could hardly keep her eyes open. "I don't think I want a story tonight, Daddy."

"Well, we can read a short one anyway," Ross said, moving to take her hand. "But if you start snoring, that's it—I stop reading..."

Kimberly giggled and stomped her tiny foot. "Stop teasing me, Daddy!" She paused and grinned at Linda. "Good night, Linda!" Kimberly turned, and then came back to kiss Linda on the cheek.

Touched by the spontaneous gesture, Linda kissed her back. "Good night, honey," she said. "Sleep well."

When Ross returned, they got back down to work. Both were determined to finish the paperwork that evening so they could have the rest of the weekend free.

That was not an easy chore. The downside of all the new business was the amount of paperwork it generated. Ross and Linda had to redo all their accounts, set up the paperwork on employee benefits, and adjust the food and supply orders.

It was eleven by the time they had finished. As they cleaned up, Linda's stomach grumbled loudly. He grinned, refusing to do the gentlemanly thing and pretend he hadn't noticed. "I'm hungry, too," he admitted, laughing. "What do you say I fix us both a sandwich?"

Now that their business was finished, Linda was reluctant to stay. "I don't want to put you to any trouble."

"It's no trouble." Giving her no further chance to beg off, he led the way to his kitchen. "Have you ever had a Philadelphia steak sandwich?" He slanted her a quick glance over his shoulder. "No? Well, then let me introduce you to some back-East culture. I promise you, you're in for a treat." His eyes scanned her trim figure laughingly, as he added, "Your waistline might not thank me, but I assure you your tastebuds will."

Linda laughed at his self-assured statement, the way he was highlighting their cultural differences in a kind of East-meets-West comedy routine. "Is that a fact?"

He favored her with a mock smile. "Yes, ma'am."

Fascinated by the ease with which he moved about the uncluttered kitchen, she watched as he put Italian bread in the oven to brown and fried paper-thin slices of sirloin steak in a cast-iron skillet anointed lightly with olive oil. Delicious aromas were filling the kitchen. "You're very competent here," she said.

"I always have been. I did most of the cooking when I was married."

"By choice?" As liberated as men were supposed to be these days, Linda didn't know many men who could prepare more than a couple of special dishes.

He nodded. "I always liked to cook, even when I was a kid. I also liked to eat, and to be perfectly honest, my mother wasn't much of a cook. Neither of my parents were. They were both more interested in what went on in their jobs as government researchers."

Somehow that fit. She could also see where being the child of career-minded intellectuals would've helped Ross to become conservative and professional himself.

"Were you an only child?"

He shook his head, his blond hair gleaming in the soft kitchen light. "No, I have a younger brother. I see him a couple times a year."

"Were you close to him, growing up?"

Ross nodded, and looked faintly troubled. "But we were rivals, too, since we were only two years apart." He shook his head, reflecting. "It probably would have been better if one of us had been a girl—then the two of us wouldn't have been so ripe for comparisons. As it was, he was always walking in my shadow, you know? Teachers, especially, had a hard time seeing us as two very different people."

Linda knew how that felt; it seemed as the youngest of three she'd had two histories or prior performances to live up to, even when she was considered the pampered, charming Harrigan. "What does your brother do now?"

Ross didn't try to hide the note of brotherly pride. "He's an airplane pilot for a commercial airline. Mostly flies the international routes. He's not married and seems to have absolutely no intention of settling down."

Ross's brother did sound very different, Linda thought. "I know what you mean," she said finally. "My two older brothers were always very competitive when they were growing up." Only recently had they evolved beyond the expectations put on them as kids. She looked at Ross curiously, feeling suddenly as if she could drown in his expressive eyes. "Was it hard for you, being older?" she asked softly.

Ross shrugged. "In certain ways. An awful lot was expected of me, but I got a lot of attention and tender loving care to make up for it." As Linda continued to watch, he added sliced onions to the meat sizzling in the skillet, then topped it with the cheese. As soon as it had melted, he slid the gooey concoction onto the toasted Italian bread. "Now, aren't you glad you stayed?"

"It looks wonderful," she noted happily.

They ate in the family room, and when they were finished, Linda sighed and stretched lazily on the comfortable divan, closing her eyes. "I'll be working off the calories all week."

Ross groaned. "Me, too, but it was worth it. I haven't done this in, well, ages."

Neither had she. But it felt good, sharing a sandwich with him. She glanced at her watch, and saw it was after one o'clock. She had stayed several hours later than she had planned. And no doubt he would have to get up early with Kimberly the next morning.

"Well, I better be going." She stood reluctantly and carried her dishes into the kitchen. Ross followed.

"Thanks for coming over tonight."

She nodded and smiled. "Thanks for the sandwich." Without warning, her throat seemed very dry.

"I'll see you Monday?" His eyes remained on her upturned face.

For the barest second, she had the disturbing sensation he wanted to kiss her. Wanted to, but wouldn't.

"Monday it is," she managed finally. He was doing the right thing, keeping his physical distance. Why, then, was she so disappointed?

"How many more miles?" Dexter demanded for the thirtieth time. It was Friday morning, and they were part of a convoy of twelve cars, containing twenty-four adults and forty-seven children, on its way to New Braunfels.

Linda consulted her map. "About fifteen, Dexter."

There was a collective groan from four seat-belted children in the car. Linda looked back at Bethany, Laura and Dexter. Kimberly was wedged in the middle of the front seat, between Linda and Ross. "It's not very far, honest. Why don't we see who can count the most cows?" Cattle ranches abounded in this part of the state. In fact, that was about all they'd seen since they'd left Austin an hour earlier.

"Okay." Behind them, the children started counting.

Ross, his eyes on the road, said to Linda in a deadpan voice, "I think I'm beginning to know the real meaning of a long day."

She laughed. "Cheer up. I know you're anxious to see the park," she teased back warmly, pretending to misunderstand. "But we'll be there soon, I promise."

"Are we really going to eat sausage and dance the polka?" Kimberly asked, her green eyes wide with anticipation.

"And a lot more, too," Linda promised. She turned around to the other children. "Who wants to count to ten in German?... That's right," she said as Dexter began quickly, his excited voice ringing out the numbers. "... *eins* ... *zwei* ... *drei* ... *vier* ..."

By the time they'd reached New Braunfels, the children had gone over not only their numbers in German, but the rudimentary phrases for "please" and "thank you," and "good morning," all of which they planned to use at the festival.

Upon arrival, the group congregated just inside the Landa Park grounds. The children were instructed to stay together at all times. For the first time, Linda noted that Dexter looked a bit daunted. He stood next to Ross and grabbed onto his hand. "I'm not gonna run off," the little boy mumbled, hanging on to Ross for dear life, as he viewed all the activity.

"Boy, am I glad to hear that!" Glenna remarked in Linda's ear. "Because the one thing we don't need today is a lost child."

Kimberly held on to Ross's other hand, looking a little bit daunted herself. "I'm not going to run off, either."

"Don't worry guys, I'll protect you," Ross said happily.

Aware the group was anxious to get started, Linda addressed them briefly. While she talked, she noted that Tad's mother, Wendy, was among the chaperons. She was glad, because she knew Tad hadn't seen much of his mother lately, what with her working and studying. This time together would recharge them both.

With Linda and Ross leading the way, the large group began touring the festival. They saw Polish dancers and rhythm cloggers, and a Bavarian band in the little tent. Brass bands and German folk dancers performed in the big tent. Scattered throughout the *Markt-Platz* were food booths selling everything from ham hocks and sauerkraut to *Wurststew* and Bavarian pork chops.

"Yuck! Sauerkraut!" Dexter said, spitting out his first mouthful.

Linda rolled her eyes, but refrained from commenting on his table manners this once.

Kimberly munched on her sauerkraut, a perplexed look on her face. "I like it," she said. She looked at Ross, who was shaking his head over Dexter's heartfelt complaint. "I hated it when I was a kid, too, Dexter," he said. "Why not just eat some of your sausage? And you might like the potato pancakes."

Dexter looked up at Ross. "Can I have dessert if I do?" he bargained.

Ross looked at Linda. "I don't see why not," she said. "They have some mouth-watering German chocolate cake."

After lunch, the group watched an oldtime melodrama, *Nothing But the Wurst* in the Circle Arts Theatre. Linda wasn't sure how much of the corny jokes the kids actually got, but they giggled right along with the crowd.

After that, everyone got a chance to dance the polka. And it was only when they prepared to start home again that the trouble broke out.

"I don't want to go home!" Tad shouted, stomping his foot and shaking loose of his mother's hand.

Wendy looked mortified by her son's behavior. Beside Ross, Dexter murmured, "Uh-oh." Ross held tighter to both Kimberly and Dexter.

"Tad, that's enough!" Wendy said wearily.

Linda remained where she was, as did all the other parents and teachers. No one wanted to come between mother and son.

Tad broke free from Wendy and ran back a few steps. "You never let me do what I want!" he cried. "Well, I'm not going to do what you say!"

Wendy colored, then blanched. Linda knew she had no choice but to step in and referee. "Why don't you go ahead and walk out to the cars with the others," she said to Wendy. "I'll get Tad and calm him down."

"I'm sorry," Wendy said, tears in her eyes, looking utterly baffled and horribly embarrassed. "I don't know what's come over him."

"Maybe he's just tired," Glenna put in. "None of them have had naps today...."

And yet none of the other children were acting this way, Linda thought. Not even the often trouble-provoking Dexter. As the others began to move off, Linda went to Tad, who was crumpled up against the side of a soft-drink booth, sobbing as if his heart would break. She knelt beside him and waited for the storm to pass.

When he'd finally wound down a bit, she held out her arms. He hurtled into them. "I don't want to go home!" he sobbed, sounding sleepy.

Linda stroked his hair, and brushed the tears from his dark eyes. "I know, sweetheart, but we have to. Come on, now, your mom and the other kids are waiting."

Slowly he got up. Still rubbing one fist in his eye, he let Linda lead him to the car.

"I CAN'T BELIEVE how good Dexter was today," Ross said, as he and Linda finished closing up the Center later that afternoon. All the other kids, save Kimberly, had gone home.

"That's the way he is," Glenna added, walking by with her own jacket over her arm. "The sweetest child you've ever seen in your life one moment, the worst hellion the next."

"And now you've seen him on a good day and a bad," Linda put in.

"Well, I have to admit he did seem like an okay kid this morning," Ross said. He looked at Linda. "Maybe I was wrong about him, after all. But that Tad..."

"I know. He's having problems, isn't he?" Linda sighed. "But I'm sure they'll work it out together, given time. In the meantime, I'm going to try to be extra patient and attentive to him at school, see if maybe I can't ward off some of this disruptive behavior. At least until Wendy passes her real-estate exam."

Across the room, out of earshot, Kimberly was playing quietly on the computer, trying to guide a rabbit through a maze. Ross glanced at her, a tender expression on his face. "Thanks for asking me to go along today, Linda. I really enjoyed it. The trip was a real eye-opener."

For Linda, too. It had given her a chance to see Ross in yet a different light. Protective and considerate of not just his own child, but Dexter, too—a child he hadn't had much use for at the beginning of the trip.

It was more than his kindness to Dexter, though, Linda thought. It was his relaxed manner. Not once during the whole trip had Ross tried to take charge, or tell Linda what to do. Instead, he had held back and waited, giving her the room and the opportunity to maneuver, and handle rough situations with aplomb.

He wasn't as smothering or domineering as she'd originally thought. Maybe, like the way he was with Dexter, Linda had just needed to see Ross on a good day, to balance the good about him with the flaws, to realize that although he wasn't perfect he was a man worth knowing.

"I GUESS I SHOULD'VE BROUGHT more than one umbrella," Ross lamented Saturday evening as he parked in the municipal auditorium parking lot. "Either that or dropped you off in front of the entrance."

They were attending a formal fund-raiser for a summer camp for underprivileged children. They'd received invitations a few days earlier and had decided to attend together.

Linda peered through the deluge hitting the Mercedes's windshield. "There's a traffic jam up there that'll be years clearing," she said, frowning at the uncooperative weather. "Besides, I'm not afraid of a little rain."

He sent her a concerned glance. "It won't hurt your dress, if you get a little damp?" Something was different about her tonight. She was as womanly as before, only now she was somehow more open in a way he hadn't felt before.

They were both dressed to the nines. Linda particularly looked gorgeous in a sophisticated black two-piece dress. The clinging black jersey was dusted with flecks of gold, the fabric reminded him of an obsidian night sky filled with tiny stars. An embroidered gold, bronze and sapphire blue design started at her throat, and spread in an enticing pattern over her shoulders and down the long dolman sleeves to her wrists. The top was cinched at the waist, with a three-inch ruffle below that. And the black stockings and black spike heels, when combined with the rest of the sophisticated outfit, made her look all woman.

"No," she said briskly. "A little rain won't hurt this dress. The fabric's more durable than it looks."

They huddled beneath the broad umbrella as they made the dash for the doors. Ross had been hoping the gala affair would be as special as the invitations had claimed, and he wasn't disappointed.

Inside, the auditorium had been transformed into three general areas, representing what every child needs—cultural, physical and emotional stimulation. On a stage, local musicians were performing a variety of children's songs. Linda and Ross took seats before the stage, enjoying the medleys from *The Sound of Music* and *Mary Poppins*. "Now that takes me back."

Linda sighed contentedly as the familiar tunes drifted around them.

"You saw the movies when you were a kid?"

"Oh yes, both, several times," she said with a buoyant grin. "What about you?"

"The old Elvis Presley movies were more my speed."

Linda looked at him knowingly, a devilish light sparkling in her eyes. "Let me guess. You liked the way he always got the girl."

"You've got my number." Ross smiled at Linda, liking the alluring way she wore her hair—all loose and flowing and curly.

As they strolled through the exhibits, he noticed other men turning, watching her. With effort, he forced his mind back to the conversation. "Not that I was completely anti-Disney," Ross commented as they stood and then, by tacit agreement, prepared to move on. Before he'd given it much thought, he'd put his hand on her lower spine and gently guided her in front of him when the pathway narrowed to admit only one at a time. The touch electrified him, and he dropped his hand as soon as it became possible for them to walk side by side again. Telling himself sternly he needed to concentrate more on what they were discussing than how beautiful she looked tonight, he continued, "I watched the *Mickey Mouse Club* faithfully every day."

She matched her strides to his, until they were walking in perfect harmony. "For me it was *Captain Kangaroo* and *Romper Room*." She paused and turned to face him, her dark blue eyes suddenly intense. "Were things simpler then or does it just seem that way in retrospect?"

Realizing she expected an answer, he said, "The times were simpler for us, certainly. I'm not sure they were so easy for our parents who lived in the Depression Era."

"I guess you're right," Linda said. Unconsciously, as the crowd picked up again she moved in a little closer to him. "There were probably just as many pitfalls then as there are now. We're just looking at them from a different point of view."

"Exactly."

Over the past few weeks, he'd begun to rely on her friendship, the steady companionship she provided as they worked on the scenery for the pageant, or simply discussed Kimberly's day. It was nice, being able to pick up the phone at any time and call her if something was on his mind and not feel he was intruding. True, most of the time they had talked only about business, but as evidenced by the more personal turn of their conversation here tonight, that, too, was beginning to change.

"What do you say?" Ross reached into his pocket for his billfold. "You up for a game of hopscotch?"

Her eyes lit up. She vacillated uncertainly for a minute, her eyes still locked with his. "I'll never be able to do it in these shoes." Laughing, she bent and slipped off her heels. "But what the hay..."

For the next few minutes they amused themselves hopping and jumping over the numbered board in their stocking feet. When their time was up, Ross reluctantly put his black loafers back on. One hand on his arm to steady herself, Linda slipped back into her shoes.

Ross admired the graceful way she moved.

From there, they tried out softballs and gloves—again for nominal fees that went directly to the summer camp—and then tennis rackets. He couldn't help but note that Linda handled a racket like a pro. "You must be an ace on the court."

Abruptly, she put the racket down and frowned. "Not really," she said quietly, in a way that let him know he had hit a sore spot. "Not for a long time."

He was surprised by her reaction. So much so he had to ask, "Why not?"

She shrugged and moved away, out of earshot of others. For a moment he thought she wasn't going to confide in him, but then she said, sighing heavily, "It goes back to an argument I had with my father a long time ago." She swallowed hard. "You see, athletic ability is very important to him. When I was twelve, my tennis coach told him I had the potential to become a professional tennis player."

"Really? That's wonderful."

She shook her head unhappily. "Not so wonderful. You see, I didn't want to give up my day-to-day freedom for the kind of dedication and regimented life-style that becoming a circuit pro would require. My father was very disappointed. It took him ages to get over it, and though he never spoke of it again, for a long time after that I would see the disappointment in his eyes whenever he looked at me." She turned to Ross more fully, the fingertips of her hands pressed eloquently to her collarbone. "For me, sports were recreation, pure and simple, a way to seek release from pressure. But for him, sports were his life."

Ross could see she hated disappointing her father. He had grappled with the same dread whenever he got lower grades than expected, or completely messed up in a school play. He knew how much that hurt, and his heart went out to her.

Unaware of the nature of his thoughts, she sighed as they headed toward the third and final area of festivities. "Oh, to be a child again, free of encumbrances and responsibilities..." she lamented.

As Ross recalled, childhood was not the easy street she was painting it. Unable to resist, he cupped a hand briefly around her shoulder, drawing her closer to let someone pass. In a deadpan voice, he added to her list of childhood delights. "...always having someone tell you what to do, when and where..."

Her eyes sparkling with suppressed laughter, she moved away from him again. Clearly, he thought, she was a woman who loved to be joshed. Maybe because she'd had two brothers who probably had once teased her relentlessly.

"Okay, sport," she said laughing. "Point made. Our youths weren't all beds of roses."

But maybe they would have been, he couldn't help thinking wistfully and unrealistically, if only he had known her then. What would it have been like growing up near Linda? Anything near as blissful as he was imagining? He could see her giving all the neighborhood boys a run for their money—probably loving and appreciating them, yet keeping them at arm's length.

Because as generous as Linda was, he noted dispassionately, she wasn't one to take risks with her heart. And even as he appreciated her caution, he railed against it, wondering if he would ever be given the chance he wanted with her, the chance to court her. To see where fate would lead them.

But he also knew he had to be patient, and patient he intended to be.

In silence, the two of them moved to the third area. It was decorated by professional designers and highlighted the emotional needs of children. Comfort food was featured for nominal prices, and included everything from chicken-noodle soup to milk shakes, pizza and tacos. After some deliberation, Linda and Ross finally decided on barbecued chicken and ribs, potato salad and coleslaw. They finished off the repast with tall glasses of icy lemonade.

"I don't know about you, but this has turned out to be a really fun evening," Ross murmured once they had finished their dinner and resumed the last leg of the tour around the domelike auditorium.

"For me, too." Linda stopped in front of a booth featuring thick fluffy quilts. All were made of soft fabric in gentle restful colors. Next to it were fabrics and furnishings in bold, bright hues, which demonstrated how to energize a play area.

Ross watched as Linda's attention was drawn to a light-blue Holly Hobby quilt with a dark rose border. "You like that?" he asked.

She nodded, entranced, "I had one on my bed just like it when I was a kid. I don't know what happened to it, though." She frowned, then shook her head, dismissing the thought. "You should buy one for Kimberly sometime, or commission a quilt for her."

"You think she'd like that?" he asked quietly, resisting the urge to link hands with Linda, to pull her closer to his side.

"I know she would, although she might need to be a little older to really appreciate it."

Ross turned to the woman manning the handmade quilt booth. "Is this for sale?" He pointed to the blue Holly Hobby. The saleslady grinned and nodded.

Long minutes later, Linda and Ross walked out of the auditorium. The rain had stopped. The air was crisp and cool, with the fresh scent of autumn. In the few hours they had been inside, the temperature had fallen dramatically, and they shivered as they climbed into his car. He started the engine and turned the heater on. Again, he had to resist the temptation to pull her into his arms and warm her properly, but remembering the unspoken restrictions of their relationship, he resisted the inclination.

The drive home was quiet and, for Ross, all too short. It started to drizzle again just as they reached her door. He pulled out his trusty umbrella, and still not speaking, they made their way to the door.

He waited, while Linda unlocked it, aware his heartbeat had picked up, that he was tense from head to foot, still wanting, waiting for a little sign from her....

She turned to him, her key still in hand. To his frustration, she didn't quite meet his eyes, but kept her gaze fastened somewhere just below his collarbone. "Well, good night," she said in a flat, emotionless tone.

Disappointment ran through him. "Good night."

His shoulders hunched slightly forward, he started to turn away, then acting solely on impulse, turned back and put the umbrella down. "Linda?"

She turned to face him, too. "Yes?" Her voice was thin and whispery as she looked at him, a pulse pounding madly in her throat. And he knew suddenly that she was as aware of him as he was of her, maybe had been since the first time they'd met.

As he continued to study her, she caught her breath and moved slightly closer. Her mouth trembled and he swore—in a mixture of frustration and acceptance of his own need. "I didn't expect this to happen," he said harshly, moving closer until they were separated by less than an inch, "but I'll be damned if I can help myself."

There was no other choice, he thought, not when she was looking at him that way. As if she wanted, but was afraid to want. As if she needed, but was afraid to need. He knew how that felt; he felt it, too.

Without warning, his arms were around her. She was against him, and then his mouth was moving lower, searching, finding, discovering. There was an instant's resistance on her part, then she softened and melted against him, surrendering to the passion driving and haunting them both.

He'd never kissed a woman who was so soft, so giving. He'd never felt this hot, maddening surge of need. He'd never touched so tenderly before, or so badly wanted to give pleasure. His hands coasted lower over her back, finding and molding against him the supple lines of her spine, her slender waist, her slim hips. She moaned, her breasts brushing the front of his pleated shirt. The softness of her body against the starched barrier drove him mad, made him want to touch her more.... But he knew it was impossible. They were on her doorstep. She might want him now, but if he persisted, she would hate him later for demanding too much of her too soon, and that he couldn't bear.

Reluctantly he let the kiss dwindle, to a soft halt. Ever so slowly, he lifted his head and stared down into her eyes. They were bright, luminous, first full of wonder, then questions. And finally, clouded with confusion and indecision. And suddenly he knew he didn't want to talk. Not then, not when there was a chance she would reject him.

Swiftly he stepped back and picked up the umbrella. Not giving her a chance to speak again, he disappeared into the blackness of the night.

LINDA WAS STILL standing there, her mouth tingling, her body aching, as Ross drove away. She watched until he was out of sight, then stepped into her house and shut and locked the door behind her. What had come over her? Why had she let that happen? But she knew, if she were honest with herself, she had invited it.

Beginning something with Ross was crazy. Foolish. She wasn't a stupid woman. She wasn't reckless. And yet here she was, flirting with fire. Again.

Chapter Six

"Give me that. It's mine!"

"Is not!"

"Is too!"

"Is not!"

"Tad, Kimberly," Linda admonished, then walked over to break up the battle. She gently confiscated the stuffed frog they were fighting over. "We share toys at school—we don't fight over them."

"Yeah, but I had it first!" Tad grumbled. He faced Kimberly, furiously. "She just walked up and grabbed it from me."

"He wasn't even playing with it. He was playing with the blocks!" Kimberly pointed to the block tower to their left, nearly two feet high.

Linda knew better than to take sides in petty arguments, even if Tad did seem more at fault than Kimberly in this instance. The truth was that neither was an exemplary student when it came to sharing. Linda had every faith they would get there, but it would take practice on their part, firmness and diligence on hers, to make it happen. "The frog is going back on the shelf for the rest of the play period," she said. "Now

I want you two to apologize to each other and call a truce."

Tad glared at Kimberly. Kimberly glared back. Linda waited while the rest of the class grew silent. "Sorry," Tad said finally. He extended his hand.

Kimberly barely touched her hand to his. "Well, I'm not. You're mean!" Before Linda could react, Kimberly stomped past Tad and kicked over the tower he'd been painstakingly building for the past hour. As the wooden blocks crashed to the floor, Tad let out an enraged howl and went at Kimberly, both fists flying. Linda intercepted him in the nick of time. The troublesome behavior was not typical for either child. Still, it had to be dealt with.

"I want to call my daddy! I want to go home!" Kimberly shouted.

"You can talk to your daddy later, Kimberly. Right now you have something more pressing to do. You have to pick up the blocks you kicked over."

Kimberly stared at Linda in mute anger. "I want to go home," she repeated, tears gathering in her eyes.

Linda refused to be swayed. "And you will go home—at two o'clock, the normal time, when Mrs. Delancey comes to get you."

The rest of the morning passed without incident. Linda kept her class busy with an art project and outdoor games. Throughout, and even into lunch and the rest period immediately afterward, Kimberly continued to sulk. So did Tad.

When Mrs. Delancey arrived to pick up Kimberly, Linda pulled her aside and explained briefly about the fight, reassuring her that the stormy mood would pass. Kimberly went to her cubbyhole and got her backpack and jacket. She stuffed her artwork in her backpack. "I'm glad I'm going home and I'm not coming back!" she announced, glaring at Linda.

The two left. Tad wasted no time in coming up to her and tugging on her sleeve. "Is Kimberly going to come back?" he asked worriedly.

Linda smiled. "Yes, she will. You'd miss her if she wasn't here, wouldn't you?"

After a moment, he nodded. He said nothing more but remained next to her in an uncharacteristically clingy way.

Linda pulled up two chairs and sat down, patting the seat next to her. Tad slid into it obediently. There was modeling clay on the table in front of them, and Linda handed him a lump, took one herself and began fashioning it into the shape of a star. "Something on your mind? Everything okay at home?" Come to think of it, Linda realized, she hadn't seen his mother much of late. Wendy had been in a hurry to pick up or drop Tad off.

Tad's lower lip stuck out unhappily. "Mommy's gone a lot. I have a sitter almost every night now." Keeping his eye on his clay, he pounded it into a flat, round circle. And then pounded it some more, adding angrily, "I can't ever do what I want!"

Linda realized that Tad lacked the good, secure feeling a child had if given plenty of attention from a loving parent. But Tad's parents had divorced, and then his mother had spent all her time scraping together enough money to feed and clothe him. Now she had an opportunity to better both their lives, but it was costing her and Tad more than she knew.

And yet, Linda wondered, remembering what a loving mother Wendy had been in the past, what choice did the woman really have? And what path should Linda, as Tad's teacher and someone who cared about him deeply, take? If she said something to Wendy, she would only be adding to the pressure Wendy already felt. And yet if she didn't say anything, wouldn't it be like condoning Wendy's obvious neglect of Tad's emotional needs?

Linda decided she needed more information about Tad's home life before she could figure out what to do. Keeping track of the expressions on Tad's face with her peripheral vision, Linda continued to look down at the clay in front of her. "Do you like your sitter?"

"She can't cook good, like my mom." Without warning, he tore up his piece of modeling clay, and when it was separated into odd sections, started pounding it flat all over again. "I wish my mommy could be there to tuck me in."

Linda was silent a moment, hearing the hurt and loneliness in Tad's voice. No wonder he had started to bully the other children, insult them, provoke fights. He had a lot of anger stored up inside, and nowhere to vent it. He only knew he felt bad all the time. And no child should have to feel that way. Still unsure what she could do for Tad, Linda questioned him further about his mom. "Is she studying hard?"

Tad nodded, and heaved a beleaguered sigh. "She reads her books all weekend. All the time." He spoke as if underlining the last.

"I see." Linda made a triangle, then a square. "That won't go on forever, you know. As soon as she gets comfortable in her new job, she'll have more time to spend with you."

"I hope so." Tad sighed again. His troubled look fading, he lifted up his clay for her to see. "Do you like my flower?"

Linda was glad he had identified it as such, sparing her the mystery. She smiled. "It's great."

They continued to work in silence for several more minutes. Tad seemed to feel better after talking to Linda about his problems, and for that she was glad.

Well, she knew what was bothering the little boy now. He missed his mom and was angry about all the changes in his life. Then she wondered what was bothering Kimberly. Was it something simple, like learning to share, or something more complex, which she and Ross had both missed?

Linda decided to think about that later, and to her relief, the rest of the afternoon passed smoothly. They finished the day with a brief staff meeting to discuss plans for the upcoming Thanksgiving pageant.

"I think we should have the entire meal catered," Helen Masterson said. "Really, it would be so much simpler."

"But more expensive," Linda pointed out, thinking that families like Tad's and Dexter's might have trouble paying for the meal if a meal ticket of seven dollars a person was charged. The main goal of the Thanksgiving feast they were planning was to get all the parents and children together.

"Well, don't ask me to cook," Glenna said wearily. "Martin says I'm no good at it."

At that all the women's heads lifted. They stared at Glenna in collective dismay. "You shouldn't let him talk to you that way," Linda said, anger bubbling up out of nowhere. "No man, not even a husband, has a right to put down his wife!"

"Linda's right. Martin has a heck of a nerve," Helen Masterson put in.

Glenna looked torn between her own anger at having been judged a poor cook and her equally strong desire to defend her husband. "Well, he did have a point," she said slowly at last, biting her lip. "I've burned every meal this week."

"You mean you've cooked every meal?" Linda asked, aghast.

"Sure. I get home first," Glenna answered naively, for once looking almost younger than her twenty-one years.

The rest of the teachers, all of whom were or had been married, moaned. "Start training Martin now," Helen advised.

"Otherwise it'll be too late," said Shana, the newest teacher on Linda's staff, and the teacher of another class of four-and-a-half-year-olds.

"They're right," Linda said. She knew from personal experience that if Glenna didn't insist on being treated equably now by her husband, it would never happen. In fact, as in her own case, it might get worse as years passed. And the love Glenna had for Martin was worth fighting for. "Make Martin do his half of the cooking, and don't let him put you down. Not ever. You've tried, and that's all that counts. Now back to the issue originally under discussion. The Thanksgiving feast. I think we should hire caterers to cook the turkey, and let the school absorb the cost. Side dishes and salad can be brought by the families.

That way we can have a great hot and cold buffet, with not too much work or expense."

There was a murmur of approval around the table. Several small matters were discussed and then the group broke up, everyone eager to get home. At six o'clock Linda was the last one there. She was just about to lock up when Ross entered, looking fit to be tied. He strode toward her, his face set in an angry mask. "What's all this about Kimberly wanting to call me today? And you refused to let her!"

Linda steeled herself. It wasn't going to be easy to tell Ross his daughter could be less than angelic. "Did she tell you why?" she asked stiffly, her chin lifting.

"I don't think it's important why," Ross enunciated through gritted teeth. "If she needs me, I'm going to be here for her—it's that simple."

Linda focused briefly on the muscle working angrily in his jaw. Damn, but she hated the way he wanted to personally control and orchestrate Kimberly's life, and indirectly then, Linda's time with Kimberly at the preschool. Knowing she had to calm him down, she said levelly, "I don't disagree with you in principle."

With a rough, impatient motion he loosened the knot of his tie. "Good, because you wouldn't win if you did."

Linda moved back around behind her desk and sat down in her chair, leaning back slightly until she was comfortable. She wasn't his partner anymore; she wasn't his good friend. She was simply the director of the preschool. She would treat him the way she'd treat any other parent in a similar situation. "Did Kimberly tell you what happened?" she asked with measured, professional calm.

Ross lifted his shoulder indifferently, then, refusing to sit down, moved back until his spine rested against the far wall. "She said you wouldn't let her play with the frog."

Linda sighed. "Did she also tell you she was engaged in a shoving match over that frog with another child, and that when I reprimanded them both, Kimberly not only refused to apologize but deliberately kicked over a tower of blocks that little boy had spent over half an hour building?"

At that bit of information, the angry color left Ross's face. "No," he admitted in a chagrined tone, "she didn't."

Linda's gaze narrowed warningly as she straightened the papers stacked on her desk. "Well, next time I suggest you get the full story, including the teacher's version, before jumping to conclusions." Feeling suddenly restless, she got up and started for the door.

He followed her into the hallway, his low voice annoyed, his steps brisk and purposeful. "I still think she should've been allowed to call me."

Her chin held high, Linda kept walking. As she strode past each empty classroom she switched off the lights. Ross was right on her heels. "Your purpose in enrolling her here was to prepare her for school next year," Linda retorted. She whirled to face Ross briefly, for a second letting go her own anger and resentment. "Kimberly won't be able to phone you should she be in trouble then. She shouldn't be allowed to get her daddy to run interference for her now."

Her voice and manner softening, Linda continued, "Kimberly has to learn how to share toys and follow direction. She and she alone is responsible for and accountable for her own behavior. She won't learn that if she thinks her daddy can bail her out without consequence every time she's rude or sullen."

Ross was silent. He was beginning to come around, but she could see he still wasn't completely convinced. Determined to make him see the wisdom of her actions, Linda went on, "Of course if Kimberly's sick or hurt or scared, it's something else entirely. But if the request comes as part of a power play, or a temper tantrum, the answer will always be no. She was testing me, Ross, and testing the limits of the school."

She flashed him a wide grin and he returned her smile sheepishly. "I'm sorry. I guess...she's had such a tough time of it...I'm sure if she hadn't endured a move recently..."

Linda knew that Kimberly would have exhibited this behavior regardless. It was her nature—bright, inquisitive, stubborn and strong-willed. "You won't do her any favors by coddling her, Ross." If he continued to make excuses for Kimberly, to let her get away with murder, then he would have a problem.

His brow furrowed and he glared at her, seemingly as annoyed with himself as he was with her and Kimberly. "You think I'm being overprotective again?" His voice was silky with challenge. One part of him both resented and disagreed with her assumption. The more logical part of him, the cool businessman accustomed to dealing with people in all sorts of trying situations, knew she had a point.

"Yes, I do."

He frowned and looked away. When he turned back to her, he eyed her critically. "Spoken like the true baby of the family," he muttered critically.

"What?" She stared at him incredulously.

"I can't help but think you're identifying a little too closely with my daughter, Linda."

"I beg your pardon?" she said stiffly.

"That you're erroneously drawing comparisons. As the baby of your family, you probably were unnecessarily coddled and hence knew instinctively if you behaved in certain ways you were bound to get what you wanted, if not from your parents, then from your brothers."

"And I suppose with Kimberly it's different?" Her stunned, angry voice ricocheted off the corridor walls.

"Yes. Kimberly deserves to be sheltered." He spoke as if underlining every word. "Whether you acknowledge it or not, Linda, she has been through a lot."

More than she ever had, his tone implied.

Linda didn't doubt that was true. She also knew Ross's blindness to his daughter's shortcomings was a trait most parents shared. As a first-time father—and a single parent—he was bound to be worse than more experienced parents. Regaining her composure with effort, she instructed sternly, "Her refusing to share toys isn't because of the move or the loss of her mother, Ross. It's because she's never had to do so before."

Again he fell silent. "Maybe you're right," he said finally, looking a little embarrassed at his emotional outburst, at his failure to think things through or question his daughter's story first.

"I know I'm right," Linda retorted crisply. If she was wrong, she wouldn't be afraid to admit it.

"So what next?" At last, he was ready to accept advice.

Linda shrugged, not expecting any disasters. "Tomorrow is another day. She'll be fine."

For a moment Ross still looked troubled. "And if she's not?" he asked.

"I'll talk to her."

He was silent again, thinking. Linda grabbed her jacket and carryall, and started for the front door. Ross walked beside her, his brow furrowed. "Why not talk to her tonight? She's pretty upset."

That, Linda didn't want. Kimberly had enough to deal with just settling into school without carrying a grudge, or feeling extraordinarily persecuted.

Furthermore, Linda had never been one to endorse allowing the sun to set on your anger. She knew Ross was right. It was best they get this totally straightened out now, so that no hard feelings lingered. It was also important that Kimberly realize she couldn't pull the wool over anyone's eyes, or get away with bad behavior without facing both Ross and Linda. "All right. I guess I could follow you home and speak to her now."

He heaved a sigh of relief. "Thanks. You're a real lifesaver. I don't know what I'd do without you."

At this moment, Linda thought wryly, she didn't either.

KIMBERLY WAS IN THE BACKYARD playing in her sandbox when Linda arrived. Deciding there was no time like the present, Linda sat down beside her. "Hi."

Idly, she picked up a handful of sand and let it sift through her fingers.

"Hi." Kimberly's tone was sullen. She kept her eyes stubbornly on the dump truck she was playing with.

"Feeling better?" Linda asked gently.

Kimberly shrugged noncommittally. Then suddenly she was on the verge of tears. Still, she refused to speak.

Seeing how much the little girl was hurting, Linda felt her heart go out to her. It was easy for her to see now why Ross had acted so protectively. He no doubt thought Linda had broken his child's heart. "I'm not mad at you, you know," Linda continued softly.

Kimberly looked up, checking out the sincerity of that statement.

"Is everything okay?" Linda continued, picking up one of the shovels and a bucket and ladling sand. "Anything you want to talk to me about now we're alone? About school or the other kids?"

Kimberly took a moment to think about that. When she spoke again, her lower lip was thrust out truculently. "The boys won't let me play with them," she reported grumpily. "And they get too rough."

"I know." Linda sighed. It was amazing to her that the battle of the sexes started at such a young age. "Some of them will outgrow it," she said soothingly. Unfortunately some wouldn't, despite the best efforts of Linda and other teachers. "You like playing with the girls, though, don't you?"

Without hesitation Kimberly nodded. "Yes, but sometimes Bethany and Laura won't do what I say!" she finished on an irritated breath, slapping her shovel on the sand for emphasis.

"Oh, I see." Linda put down the shovel and bucket and dusted off her hands. "Do you think they should... always do what you say?"

Kimberly paused, her nose wrinkling. "Well, yes," she said finally.

"What if they always wanted you to do what they said?"

"They do."

"Do you always do it?"

"No."

"Then why should they always do it?"

Kimberly was silent, mulling that one over. Linda could see she was gaining ground, and being careful to contain her excitement, she continued gently, "Nursery school can be a lot of fun, Kimberly. You learn new things, and you get to do them, too. But it's also hard, because you have to learn how to share and follow directions. Sometimes that's very hard, isn't it?"

Kimberly nodded, still distressed, but grateful that Linda understood.

"And sometimes I may have to tell you when you're doing something wrong, but it doesn't mean that I don't care about you, Kimberly. Because I do care about you." She held out her arms, and Kimberly tumbled into them. They hugged each other for several long, satisfying minutes.

"You were great with her—thanks," Ross said when Linda went back inside.

"It's going to take time, Ross, but she'll adjust to the school environment. Kids are remarkably adaptable.

Aware they were alone and, suddenly feeling nervous, Linda looked around for her purse. "Well, I'd better get home."

He gestured toward the dining-room table, where an extra place had already been set. "Stay for dinner. We've got plenty." Linda thought of the way Ross had kissed her the other night and then walked off, without giving either of them a chance to discuss it. She thought of her own tumultuous feelings. Yes, she had responded to his kiss, responded wildly, but that didn't mean she wanted it to happen again. In fact she wanted to pretend it had never happened.

She looked up at him, trying to think of a suitable excuse that wouldn't involve a discussion of that kiss. Unfortunately, none was immediately forthcoming. And by then Kimberly had taken up the cause.

"Oh, please, Linda! Please stay and eat with me and Daddy!" she said, rushing in through the patio doors. "I'll be good. I promise!"

Linda grinned down at the vivacious little girl, who had wound both of her arms around Linda's legs. There was no way she could say no to that cherubic little face. And the aromas from the kitchen did smell heavenly. "Okay," Linda said. "You've talked me into it."

The next two hours passed quickly. As was her custom, Mrs. Delancey joined them for the meal, and the four enjoyed a leisurely repast, with much laughter and inconsequential conversation. Afterward, Ross went upstairs to supervise Kimberly's bath and tuck her into bed. Linda stayed to help Mrs. Delancey with the dishes.

While they worked, Linda told the older woman of their plans for the Thanksgiving feast. Mrs. Delancey had several recipes she wanted to show Linda, and the two women sat together for several minutes, going through cookbooks, comparing the various recipes for stuffing. "I hadn't thought about it," Linda said, "but it would be neat to ask the caterer to supply not only the traditional Southern corn-bread dressing, but apple-and-walnut, chestnut, oyster, and regular sage-spiced bread stuffing, as well."

Mrs. Delancey beamed. "That way you please everybody."

They talked on. Linda enjoyed the woman's company, and she appreciated the tips on how to organize the covered-dish course of the meal. When darkness fell, however, she knew she had to get going. "Call me if you think of any other ideas," Linda told Mrs. Delancey as she left the kitchen.

"I will. And thank you for helping me with the dishes, Linda. It was a nice change to have another woman in the house."

Ross fell into step beside her as she headed for the front hall. Linda would've liked to dissuade him from seeing her all the way out, but one look at the determined glint in his eyes and she knew it would be a useless effort. He wanted to talk to her and talk to her he would.

"About the other night..." Ross began as they stepped into the cooling autumn air.

Linda had been hoping he wouldn't bring that up. She didn't really want to talk about the other evening. She had been flirting with Ross a bit too much. Not too blatantly, but enough that he'd noticed. She blamed her mood on the flirtatious dress she'd been wearing, the party atmosphere of the fund-raiser. Had they been working on school business only, she told herself firmly, that kiss would never have happened. It was just...there'd been something about the suave, handsome way Ross had looked in his tux, something about the whole evening, that had gotten under her skin and goaded her to be just a bit reckless.

Now that she'd identified what had happened, she wouldn't let it occur again. Keeping her eyes away from his probing glance, she said coolly, "I had a great time, too."

He leaned against the side of her car. "That's not what I'm talking about and you know it," he chastised in a low, solemn voice.

Without warning, Linda's knees began to tremble. Crossing her arms at her waist, she said firmly, striving for a nonchalance she couldn't begin to feel, "We're both adults, Ross. We can handle a simple kiss." At least she'd thought she could. Now...she wasn't sure.

His fingertips slid under her chin, tilting up her face, so that her glance met his. "Is that all it was?" he asked softly, his disbelief in her too casual attitude evident. "A simple kiss? It felt like more to me."

And to me, too, she thought on a wistful inner sigh. "What are you saying?" Despite her efforts to keep it level, her voice trembled slightly.

His eyes darkened in triumph. "That I want to see you outside of business. I want us to...I don't know, go out to dinner or take in a movie. Date."

She sucked in her breath, stunned by what he had suggested. "No, Ross. Dating would complicate our partnership."

He exhaled an impatient breath. "Things are already complicated." His eyes clashed with hers, and seared her with their passionate and gentle intent. "We can handle it."

Try as she might, she couldn't look away from him. The truth was that the emotional side of her wanted to be with him, because he made her feel wanted. For a long time after her divorce, and even before then, she'd felt dead inside. Her teaching and close family ties had been satisfying, but not enough. She needed more out of life, someone who would support her in anything and everything she tried to do. So far, Ross had been notoriously bad at that—criticizing her, or disagreeing, never thinking she was protective enough of his daughter. "We can be friends," she said finally, "but that's all." That's all she would let it be. "No dating."

For a second, Linda thought he would argue, but he didn't. And that left her feeling even more depressed.

OVERNIGHT A BLUE NORTHER blew in, bringing with it cold, and strong winds. Linda awakened at dawn to the pounding of rain on the roof. Yawning, she got up and went out to get the paper. Water was pooled in the streets, almost level with the top of the curb in places. Down the street, a webbed lawnchair was being buffeted haphazardly along. Another neighbor's barrel planters had been knocked on their sides. She saw a stray garbage-can lid in the gutter, and a skateboard lying sideways in the grass. Pages of newspaper were flying down the street. Great, Linda thought, estimating the gusting winds to be at least forty miles an hour. If this was what was happening here, how were things at the preschool? What about the little picnic tables in the back, the ones that she and Tom had built?

Going back inside, Linda dressed quickly, got in her car and headed for the Center. It wasn't an easy drive. Her car was continually pounded by the wind and it took all her strength to keep the vehicle on the road.

At the Center her worst fears were confirmed. The sign on the front of the building had been knocked loose on one end and was flapping crazily on the roof. Out back, the wooden picnic tables had been turned upside down and tossed around. Linda wasted no time rounding them up and placing them inside the porch where they'd be protected from the wind. That task finished, her hair clinging damply to her face, she grabbed a painter's ladder, several large nails and a hammer, and strode out to the front of the building.

She was shivering as she climbed the ladder. With one hand she grabbed half of the sign. Before she could do much more than lift it in the right direction, a car pulled into the lot. Ross emerged. He looked mad as hell.

He slammed out of the car and hurried over to her. "Are you trying to kill yourself?" he demanded autocratically. "Get down from there this instant!"

"Ross—" In other circumstances, his fiercely chivalrous manner would have been almost funny. Here, today, it was anything but, and she didn't budge. If he thought he had the right to tell her what to do—now or at any other time, she decreed silently—he had a lot to learn.

"That sign's too heavy for you." As a gust of wind caught her, he reached up and grasped her waist, keeping her from taking a spill. "Get down," he commanded brusquely, obviously piqued she hadn't moved faster to obey him. "I'll fix the sign."

Linda's arms were already trembling with exhaustion and cold. Her mind and body numb, she started to do as he bid, then unexpectedly was hit with a strong sense of déjà-vu.

What was she doing? She was letting herself be taken care of again, protected. It was that failing that had gotten her in trouble for as far back as she could remember. Because along with relinquishing her responsibility for what happened to and around her, she had also in the process relinquished her freedom. Now that she had it back, she had determined she would never seek rescue again—no matter how comfortable it was to escape from life's harsher realities. And that was a promise she intended to keep, whether Ross approved or not.

She stopped where she was and glared at him in a manner that dared him to try and stop her from what she'd originally set out to do. "I can fix the sign," she informed him imperiously. "I just need you to steady the ladder."

He rolled his eyes and moaned dramatically. "Linda, for Pete's sake—"

"Just do it!" Without waiting for him to agree, she climbed back up the ladder, extracting a nail from her pocket and began hammering it in.

Ross watched from below, frustrated, furious, not understanding. It was obvious to Linda he didn't like standing by while she did all that needed to be done. Well, that was just too bad. There was only room for one person on the ladder. If anyone was going to be a passive bystander in this life, it wasn't going to be her.

Some fifteen rain-soaked minutes later, Linda climbed down. Arms clamped across his chest, Ross glowered at her. "I could have done that in about two minutes," he said in exasperation.

She shrugged, not at all impressed. The truth was she was still stinging from his quick assumption she wasn't capable of fixing the sign. "So you're faster at nailing—" she began.

He remained where he was with obvious effort. "And stronger."

She knew that was true; she didn't appreciate his pointing it out. He pointed toward the door and folded the ladder. "We have to talk. And I'd prefer to do it inside."

Linda did as directed, but only because she was too cold and wet to argue.

"You want to tell me what all that was about?" Ross said several minutes later, as they toweled off the worst of the dampness and settled down to sip hot mugs of coffee.

"I don't know what you mean." Did he have to be so patronizing?

"Then I'll spell it out for you," he replied. "Why didn't you call me to help with the sign?"

She felt herself coloring. She was so used to thinking of the school as her responsibility and hers alone, it hadn't occurred to her. "Because it wasn't necessary," she said stiffly. "I knew I could do it."

He lifted a dissenting brow. "With much difficulty."

The color in her cheeks deepened. He seemed to think she'd made a fool of herself in merely trying to be independent. "So?" she retorted coolly.

He put down his mug with a thud and crossed to where she was seated. "So why are you trying so hard to prove you're tough? Okay, I understand, kind of, your not wanting to bother me so early in the morning for something you felt you could handle yourself, but why didn't you let me take over once I got here? What are you trying so hard to prove?"

Unwittingly he'd tapped into a very sensitive area. "Because maybe I do have something to prove—not just to you but to myself," she said softly, her mood changing. Suddenly she knew she owed him an explanation, difficult as it might be to give. "You see, I've been dependent on other people almost all my life. My parents and my brothers were all very protective. So was my ex-husband. My family still is. I used to like that."

At her reasonable tone, he sat down next to her. "But now you don't?"

For a moment, she felt almost too choked up and emotional to talk. "It got to the point where I felt smothered," she admitted finally. "And helpless. Things I should have been doing on my own, I avoided. I...I don't want to fall back into that dependency trap. Although sometimes I admit I'm tempted. Like today. It would have been easier to let you handle the heavy work, or call someone else in to do it. But that would've been silly because I knew I could get the sign back up. And maybe, just maybe, I needed to prove that to myself." She was an adult, fully capable of managing her own life. She didn't want or need anyone running interference for her anymore.

"Yeah, I guess you did prove that, all right," he said. He shifted restlessly on the chair, and his thigh nudged hers in the process. "I have to admit I didn't like feeling helpless, either."

She took another deep swallow of coffee and let the warmth fill her. Now that they'd both calmed down, it was beginning to help, the process of confiding in him. "I like being in charge, not just of the preschool, but of my own life."

"I can see that," he said softly. They turned to face one another. His hand moved to cup her face. He gently smoothed the wet strands of her hair from the curve of her cheek. "I'm sorry I snapped at you," he said finally. Then he stood up. "But don't expect me to support you when you're doing something foolhardy, because I won't."

Precisely what Linda had been afraid of. Ross still thought he knew what was best for her, better than she did. Until he believed the reverse was true, heart and soul, nothing more than a problem-fraught friendship and business partnership would ever be possible between them.

She shot him a hostile look. He finished his coffee in one long gulp, then put the cup aside. "I've got to run. I need to be there when the bank opens this morning."

Angry beyond words, Linda didn't do anything to stop him. And she was still telling herself she was glad to be rid of him, very glad, when the first of the kids started arriving at the preschool an hour later.

Wendy came in first. "What a day!" she said, putting down her umbrella so she could help Tad off with his raincoat.

"Hi, Tad," Linda said, ruffling his dark hair. "How are you this morning?"

"Sleepy."

Grumpy, too.

He glanced around. "Am I the first one here?"

"Yes, you are."

His eyes lit up. "Can I play on the computer until everyone else arrives? That Maze Craze game you got for it is so neat!"

"Sure," Linda said, glad to see him perk up. Wendy kissed him goodbye and Tad ran off to play. Linda took advantage of the quiet moment to ask Wendy how things were going.

"Great! I found out yesterday that I passed my real-estate exam. And now that I'm licensed, I can start selling houses!"

"That's wonderful," Linda said. "I know Tad has really missed you."

"I know." Wendy's expression was laced with regret. "I haven't been able to give him much quality time lately."

Or much time at all in Tad's opinion, Linda thought. "Can you remedy that?" she asked.

"Maybe. I'll try. Although for a while my hours with the real-estate company are set. Why, has he been bullying the other kids?" Wendy asked, disturbed. She had been very upset the last time Linda had to talk to her about Tad's moody behavior.

Briefly Linda explained about Tad's altercation with Kimberly the previous day. "I think they're both okay about it and will get along fine today, but I did talk to Tad, about how he was feeling in general. He really needs some extra doses of tender loving care from you, Wendy. Believe me, I know how busy you are, and I'm not trying to make you feel guilty."

"Well, that's what it sounds like you're doing!" Wendy countered defensively.

Too late, Linda saw she'd set the young mother off. "Wendy—"

"Look, I don't have time to discuss this now," Wendy snapped, looking even more harried than she had when she'd first come in that morning. "I'm going to be late for work." Without another word, she stormed off.

As Wendy left, Glenna straggled in. She was carrying a bunch of white and pink carnations in her hand, but she didn't look at all happy. In fact, Linda noted worriedly, Glenna looked as if she hadn't slept all night.

"Hi. Need some juice?" Linda said.

"Not even double-strength caffeine would help me this morning," Glenna moaned. She tossed the flowers onto Linda's desk, and shrugged out of her damp beige coat. Outside, the rain was still coming down in sheets.

"Martin?" Linda said, knowing they wouldn't have much time, if any, before other students and teachers started walking in.

Glenna nodded. "I swear to you the man is driving me crazy. It's like I'm suddenly living with an entirely different person. And we're fighting all the time—over things that shouldn't matter one whit! I don't know," she said tiredly, her eyes beginning to tear. "Maybe it was a mistake for us to have gotten married. Maybe we should have just had some gloriously romantic love affair instead."

"You don't mean that?"

"Don't I?" Glenna stormed back. "You see these flowers? Well, they're not from Martin! I had to buy them myself! He doesn't do anything nice for me anymore! It's all drudgery and dishes and fights over who should do the laundry." She buried her face in her hands.

Linda saw Dexter scamper in, his raincoat half-off. Linda shook her head, noting he was already stained from breakfast. "Hi, Dexter," she said. "How about hanging up your coat and going on into your classroom. You can get a puzzle down. Glenna will be in shortly."

"Okay!" Dexter dashed off. Seconds later, there was a crash and then a giggle.

Glenna winced, realizing it had been Dexter. "He just knocked over the entire puzzle rack again." She moaned. "Do you know how long it takes to put together those wooden puzzles when all the pieces are mixed up?"

Dexter giggled again, a sure sign he wasn't hurt. Then he yelled, "I'm picking them up! Okay?"

"Okay, Dexter," Linda called back, unperturbed. These things happened. To Glenna, she advised, "Pull yourself together." In Linda's opinion, it was time the young woman stopped the perpetual histrionics. "Having a fight with your husband isn't the end of the world. If he annoys you or takes you for granted, *talk* to him about it. Don't let resentments fester. And for heaven's sake, don't sit around feeling sorry for yourself when you haven't tried to fix things up."

Glenna sniffed, surprised by the way Linda had just spoken to her. "You're mad at me, too?" she asked, agog.

Not mad, annoyed, Linda thought. Disappointed. "I just want to see you happy. I want to see you work things out. I know you love Martin and he loves you." She didn't want to see Glenna's marriage end in divorce the way her own had.

"Okay," Glenna said, more subdued. She started off for her class, as a new wave of students straggled into the Center. Linda went to help the kids off with their rain-soaked outerwear. Why was it, she wondered, so much easier to solve other people's problems than your own?

She was excellent at telling Glenna and Wendy what to do. But when it came to herself—to her growing feelings for Ross, the desire simmering just below the surface, the confusion she'd felt after he'd kissed her, her anger with him when he wasn't supportive, her joy in being with him when he was—she was just a confused welter of emotions. A woman who had no clearcut path of action.

She wondered if and when that would ever change. Was she destined to have a romantic relationship with Ross? Was this what it was all building up to? Was that why he was so protective of her, so concerned about everything she did? Or was that just the way he treated everyone who came in contact with him?

Chapter Seven

Typical of central Texas weather, no traces of the storm-lashed night and morning remained by afternoon. Linda stood in the center of the fenced yard behind the school, watching over the activity of her class. The temperature still in the low fifties, they all had on jackets which were zipped up against the cold. Weather reports had predicted it would get cooler yet, with a blast of Canadian air on the way followed by more precipitation. "Think it'll snow tonight?" Laura asked Linda.

Linda shook her head. "The radio this morning said the low is only going down to thirty-eight."

Bethany stuck out her lower lip. "I want snow!" she said, stomping her foot.

Linda laughed. "Maybe next time," she said, and watched her run off to play on the jungle gym.

In the opposite corner of the yard, Kimberly Hollister milled around alone. Seeing the child's obvious pain at not being included in the impromptu game of tag Tad and his buddies were engaged in, or the play-acting at the sandbox, Linda walked over to her.

Up until recently, Kimberly had spent most of her time playing with Laura and Bethany. But the previous day the trio had had a fight. The other two girls had sided against Kimberly, because Kimberly was being too bossy, demanding everyone do things her way. Linda had known about the quarrel, although she'd resolved to let them work it out themselves. She knew that would happen in a day or two, as the three girls' tempers cooled, but in the meantime Kimberly could use some distraction. And perhaps a new playmate as well.

"Hi, Kimberly," she began cheerfully. "Everything okay?"

Kimberly shrugged aimlessly. "I guess."

She looked miserable. Linda glanced around, to see what playground equipment was free. "Want to go swing?" She needed some physical exercise after being cooped up most of the morning.

Kimberly gave the idea some thought. "Will you push me?" she asked finally, a faint ray of hope flickering in her big green eyes.

"Sure, for a minute," Linda said, smiling warmly. "Then you can practise pumping your legs, like I showed you last week, so you can swing all by yourself."

"'kay!" Kimberly's expression was markedly happier as she scampered off in the direction of the swing.

Once Kimberly was aloft, happily gliding back and forth, she started talking again. "Daddy told Mrs. Delancey the sign blew down during the night."

Linda smiled. "Yes, it did."

"And you nailed it back up all by yourself, without getting any help!" Kimberly was amazed.

Linda's grin broadened. "I did that, too."

"When I grow up I'm going to be just like you," Kimberly continued. "I'm going to be a teacher."

"Well, that's very nice, Kimberly."

"I'm going to be a nurse, like my mom," Marylou announced from the swing beside Kimberly.

"That's nice, too," Linda said, offering both girls encouragement to pursue their dreams. "We can always use lots of good nurses and teachers." Linda moved around to the front of the swings. "Hold on tight, girls, and don't swing too high," she cautioned.

"We won't!" They said in unison. Minutes later, from another corner of the play yard, Linda noticed Kimberly and Marylou were still talking and swinging. She sighed in satisfaction. Although she still had a lot to learn about getting along with other children her own age, Kimberly would make it yet. That was, if Ross didn't baby her unnecessarily, Linda thought.

To Linda's pleasure, the rest of the recess was uneventful. All the children cooperated with one another, and when their time was up, they filed back into the building peacefully. She was just passing Glenna's classroom when she saw Dexter climbing on top of a table and begin doing a reckless jig. Whirling in the direction of the laughter, Glenna frowned at the little boy. "Dexter, you know better than that," Glenna said firmly. "Now please get down. It's time for us to go to the computer lab, and unless you can behave, you'll have to forfeit your time on the computer."

"Oh, I'll be good, I promise," Dexter said, scrambling down.

Linda directed her class into their room, and began their afternoon social studies unit on Switzerland. Laura and Bethany were oohing and aahing over pictures of the snow-capped Alps, when a commotion started in the computer lab.

Linda excused herself, then headed in the direction of the noise. "What's the problem?" she asked.

Glenna whirled around, her face pale.

"I messed up the computer!" Dexter reported rather proudly. "The game just disappeared!"

Glenna gave Dexter an exasperated look and shook her head. She turned back to Linda, "I don't know how he did it, but he erased several things from the hard disk all by himself!"

"I punched lots of buttons!" Dexter reported happily. "Just like my daddy. We have a computer at home."

Gripping a child-sized chair, Glenna eased herself into it and buried her face in her hands. "You okay?" Linda asked. The younger teacher didn't look good.

Glenna nodded, her face still in her hands. She remained ominously quiet. "Just give me a moment," she whispered.

Linda turned back to Dexter, who was fast assuming celebrity status among his peers. She didn't want any of them to think this was okay. They worked on real computers, not toys, and computers deserved respect. "Now, you all know you're not supposed to punch buttons at random. We have to be very, very careful with our computers, don't we? Or else they will break and then we won't have any."

Dexter's face crumpled, as he realized neither teacher was thrilled with his accomplishment. "I didn't mean to do it," he grumbled unhappily, as if bracing himself for the lecture of his life.

Linda looked at Glenna, who still looked a little green around the gills. "How about if I have Dexter with me the rest of the day?" she said.

Glenna sighed. "I don't know—"

"I want to stay with my class," Dexter insisted stubbornly.

Linda knew that he should. "Will you be good?" she asked.

After a moment, Dexter nodded.

Glenna stood and ran a hand through her carrot-colored hair. She looked at Linda. "Conference after school?"

"Yes," Linda promised. They had to find a way to handle Dexter a little better.

As expected, Glenna came in right after closing. Her attitude was apologetic. "I'm sorry about what happened today, Linda. I had no idea Dexter was messing around like that. I was busy trying to teach Jimmy the new software, and then the next thing I knew Dexter was saying uh-oh!" She paused. "It's not that he's a bad kid. He's just..." she floundered.

"Always into something?" Linda suggested.

Glenna nodded. "That's it exactly. It's like he's running on high speed, I'm running on medium, and the rest of the kids are running a notch below me. I honestly can't keep up with him one hundred percent of the time, unless I pay attention only to him."

"And we can't have that," Linda said.

"Maybe we should ask his parents to have him tested for hyperactivity or...or blood-sugar levels, or something."

"Maybe," Linda mused, troubled. "What bothers me about this is that his hyperkinetic behavior is not consistent. I mean, sure there are times when he's impatient—rushing to unscrew paint-jar lids before we're ready to paint, or asking questions a mile a minute. And who can forget the morning he chased Kimberly with a water gun! But then there are also days when he seems quite content to play Superheroes at recess with the other boys."

"And there are also days when he's very quiet—almost in a world of his own. You know, daydreaming."

Linda laughed. "Or maybe just exhausted from running us ragged." Glenna laughed, too, as Linda went on, "I guess it could be a food allergy..." She wasn't experienced enough to be able to identify precisely what was wrong with Dexter; she only knew that something was amiss, and that for all their sakes they had better try to figure it out before it was too late. "I mean, I've read about kids who go crazy whenever they're exposed to citrus fruit or chocolate." Was it possible something in Dexter's diet was the culprit here and not Dexter himself?

"It would be a place to start, anyway," Glenna affirmed. "Shall I call his parents and set up a conference?"

"Please," Linda said. "And keep me apprised of the results."

No sooner had Glenna left for the day when Linda got a phone call from Ross. "I heard there was a little excitement today in the computer lab."

Linda grimaced. She should've figured Ross would get wind of what had happened. "Fortunately there was no damage to the computer. We reinserted the games Dexter accidentally erased back into the hard disk."

"So everything's cool there? You don't need my help?"

"No, but thanks for offering."

Ross was silent a moment. "There's another reason I called. It's about Kimberly. I want to know if something has happened at school. She seems, I don't know, unhappy. She won't talk to me much about what she's feeling or thinking. It's like there's this wall between us whenever the subject of school comes up. It leads me to think there's something going on she doesn't want me to know about. Or something worrying her."

Briefly Linda explained about Kimberly's fight with Bethany and Laura, her fledgling friendship with Marylou.

"Is Tad still giving her a hard time?"

"Yes and no. He's not real happy himself right now because his mom is still working long hours, but she just passed her real-estate exam and got licensed, so we're hoping her schedule will ease up a little."

"And in the meantime?" Ross asked. "Is Tad being mean to Kimberly?"

"No, but he's not going out of his way to be friendly with her, or anyone, for that matter. He seems to need a lot of space right now."

"Not to mention some tender loving care," Ross murmured.

He'd hit the nail on the head, and Linda was silent for a moment. Then, "I've been trying to draw him out a little at school."

"Does it help?" Ross asked.

"Yes, some. He lights up whenever he gets attention."

"I'll bet," Ross murmured thoughtfully. "You know, maybe we could give him a special part in the Thanksgiving pageant. Let him play the role of the Indian chief. Really make him feel important, needed."

"That's a good idea," Linda said. "I want Kimberly to have a speaking part, too."

"How is she doing?" Ross asked. "I mean other than this spat she had with her girlfriends."

Not as well as I'd like, Linda thought. It was as if the child had made great progress upon enrolling, then leveled off, and recently begun to regress a little.

Gently Linda explained this to Ross, finishing, "I'm not being critical, believe me. It's just that I worry about her becoming too dependent on me," Linda explained. "And it's beginning to be a pattern. Whenever she has a fight with a friend, Kimberly goes off alone. She waits for me to notice her, and then either I go to her, or she comes to me, and she'll ask me to help her swing or watch her go down the slide."

Ross was quiet, then he said, "You think she's looking for you to rescue her?"

"Yes. She is awfully timid about approaching the other children. I don't want her to use me as an emotional crutch. She needs to venture out on her own a little more."

"What do you suggest I do?"

"You might try broadening her social group a little more, maybe by inviting some children from your neighborhood over to play a little more often. That'll help her become more outgoing."

"Okay." He wanted to do whatever possible to help his daughter. "Anything else?"

Linda was glad he was being so objective now about his daughter. "Just be there for her," she advised in a soothing tone. "Ask her about school every day, and try to find out what if anything is on her mind. And then of course let me know if there's anything I need to be aware of or can do."

"Okay, I will. Now I have a favor to ask of you."

Linda knew she owed him at least half a dozen.

"Kimberly really loves working on the computer at school, and she's asked me to buy her some software to use on the computer at home. The only problem is, I don't have the foggiest notion what to buy for her."

"Would you like me to make some recommendations?"

"Actually I'd like you to go shopping with us," Ross said genially. "I've already checked. Several of the software stores are open on Sunday afternoons now. If you don't mind, we could make a day of it. Maybe stop and have an ice cream later."

"That sounds great."

"Okay. Pick you up Sunday afternoon?"

"I'll be ready."

As Linda had expected, Ross was right on time. They went to the software store on Research first. Then another in Highland Mall. It was late by the time they returned home.

"I don't suppose you'd agree to come over to my house and help set these games up, would you?" Ross asked, smiling.

Linda thought of all the late evenings he had spent painting and constructing scenery for the Thanksgiving pageant. Her decision was easy. "I'd be glad to help," she said.

As it turned out, Kimberly was an apt pupil. She quickly learned the computer games Ross had purchased for her, and was soon totally caught up in them. Linda and Ross, too, were totally engrossed; before they knew it, the light was fading in the family room. Linda glanced up and saw that it was five o'clock.

Kimberly smothered a yawn with the back of her hand.

"Gosh, it is late," Ross said.

"I'm hungry, Daddy," Kimberly said.

"No problem. I put the spaghetti sauce in the slow cooker this morning," Ross said. To Linda, "It's Mrs. Delancey's day off. She's out touring the hill country with members of her garden club."

"That means my daddy has to cook supper!" Kimberly chimed in, around another yawn. "He's a good cook, but he doesn't like to do dishes."

Ross flushed slightly and ignored the remark. "Kimberly, what do you say? Should we invite Linda to stay and have supper with us?"

Kimberly nodded. "Uh, okay."

"Linda?" Ross looked at her expectantly. He really wanted her to stay, she thought. He wasn't asking just to be polite.

And suddenly that was what she wanted, too. As nice as the afternoon had been she was reluctant to have it end.

While Ross finished the dinner preparations, Kimberly and Linda set the table in the kitchen. Suddenly Kimberly started out the door. "I'm going upstairs to look for Bear, Daddy!"

After she had left, Ross closed the distance between Linda and himself lazily, his gaze never moving from her face. Her heart was hammering in her chest as he casually took her hand in his. "I've really enjoyed being with you today," he murmured in a low, gravelly tone.

"Me, too," Linda said breathlessly. It had been almost like being part of a family. A couple. She'd seen what it could be like for them, and with the sole exception of Ross's overindulgence, she had liked what she'd seen—very much.

"Did you? I'm glad," he said softly, turning to face her, so close now that their bodies nearly brushed. She inhaled the faint spicy scent of his cologne, the unique fragrance of his skin, and felt her senses spin, her every resolve shatter. There might be good reasons for them to stay apart, but right now, she couldn't come up with a single one.

His green eyes darkening, he looked down at her, his glance warming to everything about her, and then ever so slowly his mouth lowered and touched hers. Just that swiftly, she was caught up in his spell. She was drowning and knew she couldn't save herself, didn't want to. Her limbs trembling, Linda gave in to the tender kiss and the flurry of emotions swamping her. She felt passion, she felt fear, she felt the warmth of simply being with him. Her body shuddered against his and pressed closer, the core of her, the heart and soul of her, vibrating with the equally strong needs to give and receive.

Only when they heard tiny footsteps bounding down the stairs did they snap out of it. Ross released Linda slowly, favoring her with another smoldering, heavy-lidded glance.

Linda blushed. She felt as if she were caught up in a dream, an indescribably delicious one.

Kimberly raced around the corner into the kitchen, Bear tucked under one arm. "Bear wants some spaghetti, too!" She sat him up in a chair, and pushed him in, until he was squished between the chair and the table, and held comically upright.

Ross gave Linda another glance, this one controlled, as aloof as usual. Whatever had been swirling inside him had been clamped down on. Eradicated.

"Okay, sweetheart." Playing along with his daughter, Ross got out another plate and set it in front of Bear. "But it has to be pretend spaghetti," he cautioned routinely.

Kimberly met that news with the acumen of someone long used to her father's rules. "All right," she said with a long-suffering sigh.

The meal turned out just right. From time to time Ross sent curious, almost thoughtful looks Linda's way. She lowered her glance, not wanting Kimberly to see the sparks flying between them. What had she gotten herself into? Even as she thought it, she wanted to blush again, and then was irritated with herself for behaving so transparently.

Finally the meal was over. Ross got up and started to clear away the dishes. "I'll just put these in the dishwasher and then run you home." Linda was all too aware he would have to drive her. Had she her own car, she would have bolted from his premises immediately; she felt confused and in need of time to think.

"No problem—" Linda responded casually.

"I want a story, Daddy," Kimberly piped up. Trodding closer, she tugged on his pant leg and looked up. "I want you to read to me. Remember, this morning, you promised you would read to me right after supper?"

Reminded, Ross sighed.

"I'll do the dishes, you can go read to Kimberly," Linda said swiftly. It would give her something to do, and keep Ross out of her sight while she was doing it. Then she would really have to go.

When she'd tidied up the kitchen she went back into the living room. Ross was sitting with Kimberly curled up on his lap. They were almost at the end of the story. Taking a chair opposite him, she waited until they finished. Then she said, "Ross, I've really got to get home."

He stood, his reluctance to let her go mirrored in his eyes. He looked as if he wanted to talk to her. For a moment, Linda thought about behaving recklessly and staying to hear what he had to say. So what if there were still oodles of reasons they shouldn't be together? So what if she had a lot to do before school tomorrow? She was here, now... Kimberly would be going to bed soon. They could get this straightened out, maybe even agree their few kisses shouldn't happen again...

And it was then Linda saw it, a flicker of relief on Kimberly's face, which told her more eloquently than words that Linda really had outstayed her welcome, at least as far as the little girl was concerned. "I should really be on my way," Linda said.

Ross's glance narrowed briefly. He didn't agree with her decision, but he wouldn't argue with her, either. "I understand," he said with a Philadelphian politeness that almost stung. "I didn't mean to delay you. Just let me run upstairs and get some letters I need to put in the mail. I can drop them off in a mailbox on the way home. It'll save me some time tomorrow."

While he was gone, Linda helped Kimberly with her shoes. "Are you coming to see us next Sunday?" Kimberly asked.

It was a polite question, gently voiced, but Linda couldn't help but pick up on the faintly troubled note behind it. And again, she had the feeling that as right as Ross's kiss might have felt forty-five minutes earlier, this was still all wrong.

"I'm not sure right now what my plans for next weekend are. Why?" Linda asked softly. Kimberly shrugged and didn't answer. "Do you want me to visit you next Sunday?" Linda probed.

Again Kimberly only shrugged.

"You can tell me how you feel," Linda encouraged. If there was a problem, it was better they get it out of the way now, rather than handle it at school when Linda was distracted by the demands of other students.

"I like it better with just me and Daddy," Kimberly said.

Linda reeled inwardly, feeling as though she'd had the wind knocked out of her. Well, that was certainly honest, but she had asked for honesty. More, she should have expected it, as Kimberly was too young to have developed a false cordiality. She could only say what she felt. And she felt Linda was butting in where she had no right to be.

Maybe Kimberly was right.

Ross's footsteps preceded him into the room. He had a stack of stamped envelopes in his hand. "Ready to go, ladies?" he asked briskly.

Linda nodded. Aware her emotions were in turmoil, Linda averted her glance. Kimberly leaped up with a smile, suddenly a barrel of energy. "I'm ready, Daddy! And so is Bear!"

When they arrived at her home, Linda said good night to Ross and Kimberly hurriedly, then leapt from the car. "I'll see you at school tomorrow," she said to Kimberly.

"We still need to talk," Ross said, his voice sounding a bit grim despite the overtone of pleasantness. "I'll call you," he finished softly, his low voice underscored with both a promise and a faint but steely threat.

Go ahead and call. I won't be in, Linda thought. *I can't be. I need time to think, figure out what's going on inside me.* And she knew she couldn't do that when Ross was around. He was just too distracting....

"WE'VE GOT THE RESULTS back on Dexter and you're not going to believe it," Glenna said late Wednesday afternoon, after the children had left for the day. She had just returned the call from Dexter's mother.

"He's not hyperactive?" Linda asked. Glenna looked too happy for the news she had received to have been bad, she thought.

"Not at all according to his pediatrician and the psychologist who tested him. Nor does he have any food allergies. He does, however, have an IQ that puts him in the gifted range. They discovered he can already read at a second-grade level—as a three-year-old!"

Linda's mouth dropped open. This certainly explained a lot about his behavior. His impatience, his love of creative play, his determined tinkering with the computer. "How is it that none of us knew this about Dexter?" At school, thus far, there really hadn't been a chance for Dexter to show off his reading ability.

"I don't know. Chalk it up to his being the last of six very active kids. I mean, his parents adore him, but as you know, they don't have that much time for him. Anyway, we've been given some recommendations, and one of them is that we keep Dexter as challenged as possible."

"Of course!" Linda said, her mind already speeding ahead. "We could move him up to a more advanced class, except that socially, emotionally, he's not really ready for it."

"Right. Those four-and-a-half-year-olds would walk all over him. Maybe we can just keep him going with independent projects. You know, give him more computer time and harder games to play, ones that emphasize problem-solving, and require higher-level thinking."

"That very well might do it. At any rate, it's a start, and at least we know what we're dealing with."

"Amazing, isn't it?" Glenna plopped down. "We have just identified our very first genius!"

Linda smiled. "And hopefully not our last."

"Oh, before I forget. Ross called. He says the synthetic buckskin for the pageant finally came in and he's ready to start working on those tepees. He wants you to call him to set up a time." She paused, then asked, "Everything okay with the two of you? I thought I noticed a little tension between you the past couple of mornings when he dropped Kimberly off...."

Things had been tense. Linda had been avoiding him, not giving him a chance to be alone with her. At first he'd been puzzled, then hurt, then almost angry. She knew he was bound to be annoyed with her, but in a sense that was safer than having him desire her. Because, the passion aside, there were still vast differences between them. Linda wasn't sure she wanted to get further involved with anyone who was so protective of the women in his life.

And it wasn't just that, it was Kimberly, too. Try as she might, she just couldn't forget that relieved look on Kimberly's face Sunday evening when Linda was going to go home, or the quiet admission that Kimberly didn't want her around all the time.

And she knew that Ross felt that the bond between parent and child is so strong that nothing, no one, can break it. A person would have to be foolish to get in the middle of that. And she had never been foolish.

What Kimberly needed—what they all needed—was time. Time to think things through, to figure out what was right. And right now, judging from the way Ross had looked at her that morning, that could only be accomplished if she maintained her physical distance from him a while longer.

Unfortunately for Linda, there was still the pageant and all the attendant preparations to take into consideration. But again, there was nothing she couldn't handle alone. "Would you do me a favor and call Ross back for me?" she asked Glenna. "Tell him... tell him I had plans for tonight, and um, well, I'll get back to him tomorrow." Maybe she could go over and pick up the buckskin when he was at work, construct the teepees herself, or enlist Glenna's help.

"You're sure you don't want to call him?" Glenna asked, her brow furrowing.

"Positive," Linda leapt up. Suddenly, she knew she had to get out of there. The sooner, the better.

Chapter Eight

Ross tossed his racquetball gear onto the front seat of his car and climbed in. Eight-thirty in the evening, Kimberly was asleep, Mrs. Delancey was settled before the television, her knitting in hand—and he was as restless as hell. Fortunately the health club where he worked out was open until midnight every night of the week. It had been too late for him to secure a partner, but not too late for him to get a court. He figured if nothing else he could slam the ball around on his own and work out some of his aggression.

Not that he had any reason to be feeling so out of sorts. It wasn't as if he and Linda had argued about anything. Nonetheless he couldn't shake the feeling she was holding him at arm's length, as much against her will, as with it. Or maybe he'd made a big mistake, kissing her again on Sunday.

She'd told him before she didn't want to get involved. And he'd tried to honor her wish, not pressure her. For a while, the friends-only routine had worked. But now it was getting to be a strain, because he knew now he wanted so much more from her. And unless he was mistaken, she wanted more from him, too. The only question was how to get her to admit it.

Traffic was backed up on Route 183 as he headed north. When he got to the Balcones Country Club, he turned left off the six-lane highway and took a back route through the quiet shady streets of the Spicewood subdivision, where Linda lived, to the health club in Anderson Mill. The fact he would pass Linda's home en route had nothing to do with his decision to take the time-saving detour, he told himself firmly.

He wasn't shocked to see the lights burning at her place. She often left them on while she was out, so she wouldn't have to come home to a dark house. Nor was he surprised to see the car in the drive. It was entirely possible her plans had been to go out with a friend. He was surprised, then, to see her garage door open. She was inside, alone. In jeans and an old sweatshirt, she was wrestling with three long wooden poles and a rope, trying unsuccessfully to construct a tepee for the Thanksgiving pageant.

His foot hit the brake. He'd offered to help her tonight, but she'd refused, saying she had other plans, and would call him when she was ready to start on the last of the set decorations. But she hadn't. He knew, because he had been home and the phone had been free. What kind of game was she playing?

Linda saw the familiar Mercedes station wagon park at the curb, and watched as Ross got out of the car. He was wearing shorts and a T-shirt. He shut the car door with a decisive thud and, looking anything but happy, started for her.

He knew, she thought, her heart thudding. He knew she'd misled him about her plans tonight, that she'd planned all along to work on the scenery and just didn't want to be with him.

"Hi," he said grimly.

Linda swallowed around the knot of apprehension in her throat. "Hi." She took a deep, steadying breath. "Going to the health club to work out?" she asked nonchalantly.

He nodded. "Your other plans got canceled?"

She nodded, still maintaining a death grip on the three unwieldy wooden poles.

"You should have called," he reprimanded pleasantly. "I would've been glad to help you tonight."

She shrugged, refusing to let him intimidate her with that all-knowing look of his. She was perfectly within her rights to spend the evening however she wanted. "I figured I could handle the construction of the frame alone. I guess not."

He ran a hand idly along the curve of his jaw. She wasn't sure what he was thinking, wasn't sure she wanted to know.

"Want some help?" he asked finally.

She shifted the bulk of her weight from one foot to the other. Funny, the conversation was perfectly civil—at least on the surface—yet she felt as if she were involved in a Mexican standoff. She sent him a pleasant smile. "I wouldn't want to make you late for your racquetball game."

He shrugged indifferently. The motion drew her eyes to his chest, the way the much laundered T-shirt clung to the well-defined muscles. "That's okay, I wasn't meeting anyone." Again, his voice was very civil.

Despite her effort to remain cool and collected, she began to flush. "Well..."

He continued watching her, refusing to drop his gaze, to let her off the hook. He stepped forward to lend a hand. Under his expertise, the three wooden poles came together easily. He held them, tops together, bottoms apart, while Linda got the rope and began lacing the poles together.

He watched her work. "You knew you were going to do this tonight all along, didn't you? You just said you had other plans because you wanted to avoid seeing me."

She was silent, refusing to answer, refusing to be bullied into doing what he wanted when he wanted. She had done enough of that in her first marriage.

She finished tying the knot. He let the poles go. They remained standing. "There, all done." She stepped away.

He followed her. His hand touched her shoulder. She could have jerked free and he would've let her go—she felt it in his touch. "Linda, what's going on?" he asked softly. "What's got you so upset? Was it the way I kissed you Sunday night or—?"

That, she didn't want to talk about.

She couldn't look at him. If she told him, he would think she was foolishly cautious. Yet she knew she couldn't continue to evade him without hurting his feelings terribly, something she didn't want to do.

"I don't want to come between you and your daughter," she murmured.

Ross was baffled. "Did Kimberly say something to you?"

Linda nodded and briefly explained. "When I'm with you too much, Kimberly starts to feel abandoned. Shut out. That shouldn't be the case, Ross. Maybe we're moving too fast."

He made a dissenting sound, but she overrode him. "And that being the case, I think we should cool it for a while."

His eyes narrowed as he faced her. "So rather than discuss this with me and see what I felt about it and give me the chance to put my two cents in, you made the decision on your own."

She turned away, mortified to find she was near tears. She hadn't expected to get so emotional. "I didn't want to fight about it," she said in a choked voice, walking into the garage. "I just wanted time to think."

He followed, watching as she pushed the button that activated the door. "Then you also knew I would think you were wrong," he said as the garage door slid closed, sealing them in the cluttered room. "Because something is happening here, Linda, whether you want to admit it or not. Our feelings for each other are growing. They're changing. And we need to admit it, talk about it."

Did they?

Feeling penned in, she opened the door to the house and went inside, leaving him to follow her. Silence fell between them. She knew she had to explain the reason behind her fears. "You've been alone a long time, Ross, and so have I." She stood with both hands splayed on the kitchen counter. She swallowed hard, her gaze pinned on the gleaming white formica. "The solitude can make you reckless." How well she knew that. What other explanation could she give for the wholehearted way she had responded to his kisses, the way she wanted to feel his arms around her even now?

He placed his hands on her shoulders, gently guiding her around to face him. When she did as directed, he didn't step back, and they were standing thigh to thigh, chest to chest, their bodies touching in one warm, tensile line. "You would never be a one-night stand for me," he whispered huskily.

Right then, she just felt mixed up. As if she might be falling for Ross in every major way. And afraid—afraid it wouldn't work out, afraid it would, and that she'd end up in a man's shadow again, the same way she had before. Yet the idea of simply letting go of her life, of her control and to let herself bask in his warm, attentive manner was tempting.

Not trusting herself to meet his eyes—and not kiss him again—she leaned her head against his shoulder, confessing softly, honestly, "I know that Ross. I know you wouldn't just be with me one night and walk away. But I also know when you rush into a love affair without thinking it through first, it greatly increases the odds it will end badly. And I don't want to be a one-month stand for anyone. Or a one-year stand." She paused for a breath, wetting her lips. Looking up at him, she confessed in a throaty, urgent whisper, "I'm looking for the real thing, and to find that, to develop it properly, you—we—have to go slow."

He grinned lazily, his manner all predatory male. "I can go slow," he teased, with a rapacious wink.

"Ross!" she reprimanded, blushing.

He turned serious again. "I know what you're saying, and believe me, I'm just as eager to protect myself from getting hurt as you are. But there our similar feelings end, Linda. Because I think you're dead wrong about the way you want to solve this dilemma of ours." His hands came up to lightly cup either side of her face. Eyes searching hers, he said, "Passion and love and desire are all strong emotions. Emotions too strong to be put on some kind of timetable, and neatly label and develop. Feelings happen. Romance happens." His eyes darkened and his mouth lowered. "Kisses happen..." he said huskily, touching his lips to hers for the barest fraction of a second.

At his nearness, the feel of his mouth against hers, her heart skipped a beat. And then another. "Ross..." She meant the word as a warning. It sounded like a caress.

"This happens, Linda." He lowered his mouth to hers and kissed her, lingeringly this time. "And this." He unloosened the scarf she'd tied around her hair, and removed the pins. The dark locks fell in a riot of curls around her face, over her shoulders. He wove his hands through the silky mass.

And then he kissed her again, this time giving no quarter, only taking and taking, and demanding that she take back. Linda was swept into currents too powerful to ignore, currents that were stronger and more satisfying, and more debilitating, than anything she had ever known. She felt drained. She felt alive. She felt enervated. She felt wanted, loved. Cared for.

"Now, tell me you don't want me to stay," he whispered roughly, impatiently, releasing his hold slightly.

She tilted her head back, not stepping out of the loose circle of his arms.

"Admit you missed me," he whispered again, kissing her temple, the curve of her neck. "Admit you want me to kiss you again."

She let her head drop back languorously and shut her eyes. "I missed you. And I want you to kiss me again."

"And I missed you." He drew her to him tighter, hugging her close, until she felt their heartbeats were no longer separate but one, as their souls were one.

"Kimberly..." Linda protested weakly after yet another kiss.

"She'll come around."

"If she doesn't..."

"She will." He touched her face, smoothing dark strands from her temple. "It's natural for her to be a little jealous." His lips touched her temple again. "Because she sees how much I care for you—but she'll get over it."

Linda sighed and leaned into Ross, savoring the warm, secure feeling of his arms around her. "I don't want to come between you and your daughter."

"You haven't and you won't. Even if you tried, I wouldn't let you. But my loving Kimberly doesn't mean I have to cut myself off from other adults. Especially beautiful female adults."

Linda grinned. He was right. Kimberly would adjust, given time. She'd been a fool to let anything get in the way of her blossoming romance with Ross. "What about racquetball?" She looked at his clothes.

A determined look on his face, he took her into his arms again. "Racquetball can wait," he said softly. "Tonight I want to be with you."

He took her hand. "Before I forget, I've got the material you needed in the back of the wagon. If you want, we can try to finish the tepee tonight."

"That'd be great," Linda said. "With the pageant only four and a half weeks away, I'm beginning to get a little nervous about getting everything done."

"Not to worry." He grinned reassuringly. "I'm sure we'll manage, especially if we're working together on it."

Linda grinned back, aware that he was treating her like a full partner now, rather than bossing her around. "I'm sure of it, too," she said.

Over the next few days, Linda spent a great deal of time with Ross. They finished the construction of both tepees and all the other set decorations. Glenna and Helen were writing the scripts for the children, and rehearsals for the pageant would begin the following Monday, then be held each day during social-studies class until the big event. Many of the mothers had volunteered to sew costumes for the children.

In addition to taking care of school business, Ross took pains to gradually incorporate Linda more and more into his home life. And he did it in such a way neither his daughter nor Linda could object. He'd call her up and ask her to drop school papers by his house early in the evening, or have supper with Kimberly and him—ostensibly to test some recipe for the Thanksgiving pageant, but really just to have her with him.

He did this so unobtrusively and naturally, she couldn't possibly get peeved. And his strategy was working. After another week and a half, Kimberly was not only getting used to seeing Linda at her home almost every day, but welcoming, sometimes even suggesting her presence.

Such as the night she asked Linda to stay and help her make her father's favorite dessert.

"How much water?" Kimberly asked, her eyes serious. She was standing on a chair, an apron wrapped around her middle.

"Two tablespoons." Linda handed her the appropriate measure and watched as Kimberly filled the spoon with water.

The more time she spent with Kimberly, the more she noticed how alike Kimberly and Ross were. Both were strong-willed, determined to have their own way, and yet vulnerable, too, with an enormous capacity for caring. Both demanded a lot of those close to them, but both gave a lot in return. "That's good," Linda continued. "Now sprinkle it over the top of the apple slices—great, that's perfect." She smiled encouragingly.

"Now what?" Kimberly said when she'd finished. She beamed up at Linda as if Linda was too precious for words.

Touched by the heroine worship she saw in Kimberly's eyes, Linda reached for the crumbly mixture of flour, sugar, butter and cinnamon. "Next, we take the topping mixture we made earlier and sprinkle it over the apples." She watched as Kimberly did as directed. "Very good!" Linda said when Kimberly had finished. Kimberly really was a quick study.

"Now do we bake it?" Kimberly asked eagerly.

"For twenty-five to thirty minutes," Linda confirmed. She slid the baking dish into the oven.

Ross walked into the kitchen. Hands planted loosely on his hips, he stood surveying both women with exaggerated somberness. "Who's cooking my favorite apple crisp?"

"We are, Daddy!" Kimberly jumped up and down excitedly. "And it's going to be good!"

"You bet it's going to be good." Ross enveloped her in a bear hug, then tickled her middle.

Kimberly giggled in delight. "Guess what else, Daddy? Linda said I can make an apple crisp for the Thanksgiving feast we're going to have! Isn't that neat?"

"It sure is. You're getting pretty excited about the pageant and the feast, aren't you, honey?"

Her green eyes sparkling, Kimberly nodded. "I'm even learning my lines," she said importantly. She pointed to herself. "I get to be a pilgrim lady and help feed all the Indians."

She cocked her ear as she heard the television music in the background. "*Sesame Street*'s on! Can I go watch, Daddy?" She was already wiggling out of her apron.

"Sure. Just make sure you're *sitting* on the furniture, not doing somersaults off it, okay?"

"Okay!"

Still grinning, Ross watched her scamper off. He picked up the apron and folded it neatly. "She sure looks happy." He gave Linda a complimentary look.

Linda felt a warm glow begin in her middle and spread outward. "She is. Of course all the kids are excited about the pageant. That's all they can talk about these days, and it's still three weeks away."

"That's good, but I was talking about your being here tonight," he said gently.

"Oh." Linda ducked her head shyly. "She doesn't seem to mind my presence here now."

Ross's glance darkened appreciatively. "That's because you've gone to such pains to make sure she's not just included, but appreciated."

"I care about her." More than just a student now. More like a favorite niece, Linda thought. Not that this was surprising. Her willful moments aside, Kimberly was a sweet child, very loving, full of energy and spunk. She had a lot to give, and a way of finding her way into your heart before you knew what hit you.

Ross took a peek in the Crockpot, where he had a stew simmering. A delicious aroma filled the kitchen.

"How were your phone calls?" Linda asked. While they'd been baking, he'd been in his den, conducting a little after-hours business.

"Very productive, actually."

She smiled, and began to set the table for dinner.

KIMBERLY HAD BEEN PUT to bed. Ross made a fire in the fireplace in the living room, and he and Linda sat in front of it, basking in the warmth of it and each other, sipping their liqueurs. He trailed a finger down her spine. "I'm glad we're finally spending an evening alone together," he said warmly, pulling her toward him on the couch.

In the quiet of the house, Linda gazed at him, feeling curiously replete, and yet on edge. She knew the moment of reckoning had come, that it was time their relationship moved into more intimate territory. Past time, maybe.

His mouth touched hers and she knew she didn't want him to stop, that he wouldn't stop, not until they were one. The couch was long, and he stretched her body and his the length of it, then covered her with his own. His weight was welcome.

She had known she wanted this for days now, for many long lonely nights. She hadn't known when it would happen, but now that it was, she knew the time was right. They hadn't said the words, either of them, but she knew he cared about her and she cared about him, more deeply and completely than she had ever cared about any man. He was gentle and kind and good. He had a lot of love to offer. And she had an aching need to accept it.

Wreathing her arms about his neck, she gave herself up to the sensual embrace, all too aware that when they were together like this, they ceased to exist as individuals, and became linked irrevocably as one, body and soul. It was a sensation she cherished, and one that was new to her.

His mouth was sweet, vulnerable. He showed her that need was nothing to be ashamed of, that it was all right for her to surrender herself to him, because he was surrendering to her. He kissed her as though he meant to go on kissing her forever. His fingers found the profile of her face, the slender arch of her throat, the slope of her shoulder, her trembling hands. She held him close, mindlessly returning the pressure of his mouth. Every inch of her burned; his own pulse throbbed and skidded.

His mouth didn't lessen its velvet assault, but as the minutes drew out, his kisses were first rough, impatient, then incredibly tender by wooing, by turns. When they paused long moments later to catch their breath, firelight touched the hollows of his face, and his emerald eyes held her mesmerized. She saw the capacity for tenderness in him. This is what she'd been waiting for, she thought, all her life.

And it was worth the wait.

"Linda?" he said softly.

She knew he was giving her the chance to back out, that even though he was ready for this step, he would understand and support her if she was not. That he would give her all the time in the world if that was what she wanted. But it wasn't at all. She wanted him as much as he wanted her, and tonight she would have him.

And she knew now why they were so right for one another. It was because they were different, because like pieces of a puzzle they fit together well. When she was too idealistic or flighty, he was rational. When he was too rigid, she helped him to lighten up. Together, they made a good team. They brought out the best in one another. He understood her, and she him.

"I want this, Ross," she whispered, letting him know with her eyes and the tender touch of her lips to his that it was true. "I want you." His eyes darkened and grew bold with need. Slowly, she reached up and unbuttoned his shirt. They kissed again, his hunger for her so honest, so real. Then he rolled to the side, taking her with him. He wanted her, had always wanted her, she thought, as his hand undid the zipper on the back of her dress. His eyes holding hers, he shrugged out of his shirt, then his pants. With gentle motions he divested her of her dress, the sexy lingerie. "I need you," he whispered.

She took his mouth again and again as his palm teased the length of her. And then she felt a helplessness invade her bloodstream, more potent than any drug. Only this time she wasn't afraid of the feeling. She cherished it the same way she cherished him.

"I need you, too," she whispered back, touching her lips to his jaw, his cheek, his mouth. His beard was abrasive, and the intoxicating scent of his aftershave clung to his jaw. His body was so hard, so smooth, so incredibly virile and male. She wanted to know all of him, to feel the need, to race with the pleasure, and find the pinnacle awaiting them both.

Lacing his fingers behind her neck, he lifted her lips up to his. Accepting, relishing her vulnerability, the fierceness of his possession, she let her thighs fall open so that the hard-muscled warmth of his legs were between them. His hands found her breasts and fierce shudders shook her body. The tight ache in her nipples grew, assuaged only slightly by the warmth of his mouth. She rocked against him imperceptibly, losing herself in the tightening pressure, the growing need. His hands drifted lower, searching, finding, demanding more. Desire bloomed and grew inside her, intensified by each loving touch, making her body feel open and empty, making her his. "Ross," she whispered, thinking, *I need you. I love you.* "Oh, Ross."

"Don't stop touching me," he whispered raggedly. "You feel so good, so good." She touched him again, not as shyly. And then something changed, everything changed. He looked at her like he wanted to consume, take over, possess. His mouth covered hers and didn't let go, not once. She found herself holding on, holding him close, holding him tight. And then he was taking her to places she had never been, had only dreamed about. Slowly, then ever faster... the blending of bodies became the blending of souls.

SHE LAY AGAINST HIM, her face burrowed in the warmth of his hair-whorled chest. She could hear the steady drumming of his heart beneath her cheek. She felt the enveloping strength of his arms around her and cuddled even closer, content to simply lie beside him and watch the burning embers of the fire.

"We should move," she murmured finally, although she didn't know where she would find either the strength or the will.

"To a bed," he agreed, not moving.

She smiled. Her lips touched his skin and she followed that with a kiss. "Okay, I'll race you." She stifled a yawn, aware she'd never felt cozier or more cherished than she did at that moment. Never had she felt so utterly content. "Ready—" she yawned again "—set... go!"

Again, neither moved.

Laughter rumbled up from deep inside his chest. "Guess that settled it then. We both win."

"Not lose?" Puzzled, she propped her hand on his chest, and her chin on her hand, so she could better see his face.

He smiled, his expression one of glowing affection. "How could I lose when I have you in my arms, and vice versa?" His low voice deepened even more. He took her face between both his hands and guided it nearer. "In case I forgot to tell you earlier," he whispered, a hint of laughter and merriment in his voice, "in case you didn't notice—" his eyes darkened even more "—I love you." And he touched his mouth to hers.

Linda closed her eyes, savoring the words, the moment, the exquisite feel of him next to her. "And I love you," she whispered back. "With all my heart and soul."

AFTER LINDA LEFT first thing in the morning—they did eventually retire to his bedroom—the rest of the day passed slowly for Ross. He went to the bank, dealt with staff problems and customers, paperwork—but his mind was on Linda. Constantly.

When he left at five-thirty, the weather had turned very cold. He looked at the sky, and realized from the dark blue-gray hue of the clouds, that another cold front was moving in.

By the time he got home, the temperature had dropped to thirty-six degrees and it had begun to rain. As always, when the threat of icy roads seemed imminent, he began to worry. Needing to reassure himself Linda was all right, he called her at her home. No answer. Figuring maybe she was still at work—she'd mentioned something the previous day about trying to get organized for the Thanksgiving pageant—he tried the school. To Ross's relief, she answered on the third ring. "What are you still doing at the Center?" he asked lightly.

"Paperwork. Trying to get everything ready for the pageant. The kids turned in their lists of who's bringing what this morning. Unfortunately we ended up

Lifetime Guarantee

with too many salads and not enough side dishes for the feast, so I'm calling a few of the parents to ask if they'd mind switching."

"Any luck?"

"So far everyone has been most gracious, but I have about fifteen more calls to go, so it'll be a while before I can guarantee a balanced buffet."

"You're going to make all the calls from the school?"

"Probably," she answered absently. "Why?"

Trying hard not to sound like a mother hen clucking over an errant chick, Ross said casually, "I just heard the weather report. The temperature is dropping. They're expecting the rain to turn to sleet by midnight." And though it was only seven o'clock now, he still worried about Linda's ability to get home safely. Not that she would probably be staying at the school until midnight...

Linda groaned. "I hope not. The one thing most Texans cannot do well is drive on icy roads. One patch of ice causes more accidents than you'd believe."

Ross's gut twisted. Fighting to keep his voice matter-of-fact, he said, "That's what everyone at work was telling me. They left early to avoid it."

"You, too, I guess?" she teased.

He didn't see anything humorous about the subject. "I didn't want to get stuck in a pile-up on the I-35."

"I wouldn't, either," she said wryly.

Ross could hear her sorting through papers on her desk as they talked. "So, in light of that, will you be going home soon?"

Linda sighed. "As soon as I can. Fortunately I don't have far to drive." In the background, the other phone rang. "Look, I've got to go, sweetheart. I'll talk to you later, okay?" Linda said.

Before Ross could respond, or offer to come pick her up, she'd hung up.

He checked the temperature. Thirty-five, and still dropping, but slowly. Which meant it would be a while before it started icing. He had nothing to worry about.

And yet he couldn't stop worrying about Linda. Dammit, he had a bad feeling about this. Decisively, he picked up the phone again and called the school. Both lines were busy. Half an hour later, he still couldn't get through. And the outside temperature had dropped to thirty-four.

Ross swore and went for his coat. He told Mrs. Delancey where he was going and that he would be back as soon as possible. To his mixed feelings of relief and frustration, Linda was still on the phone when he arrived.

Raising her brows in silent inquiry, she quickly finished her conversation and hung up. "What are you doing here?"

Glancing around, Ross saw that she'd taken one phone off the hook, probably to avoid interruption. He replaced it. Now that he was here, he found he was brimming over with anger at her careless disregard for her own safety. "I might ask you the same question," he said tersely.

She looked surprised by the rigidity of his manner, but said calmly, "I was talking to the manager of the Safeway. It took me half an hour to persuade him to give me twenty eighteen-pound turkeys at cost. That'll feed two hundred guests, don't you think?"

At that point, Ross couldn't have cared less about any of the details of the Thanksgiving feast. But to answer her question, he said, "Probably, but Mrs. Delancey would be a better judge of that than I."

"Then I'll ask her," Linda said, reaching for the phone.

Before she could so much as lift the receiver off the hook, Ross's hand had closed over hers. "No need to call her now. I'll ask her when I get home and let you know," he said as pleasantly as possible.

She looked at him again. "Okay, Ross. What's going on? Why are you here?" she asked in a mystified voice.

Ross shrugged, feeling suddenly embarrassed, and yet no less protective. "I thought I'd offer you a ride home," he said finally.

She was disconcerted. "That's sweet of you, but—" her voice faltered slightly as she stared at him, shaking her head "—I have my car here."

"I know. But, uh, the roads are starting to get bad."

At that, her face changed unhappily. "Ross, I've driven on ice before. My Honda has front-wheel drive."

Even so, Ross thought, that wouldn't save her if a big truck swerved out of control and hit her car.

"My station wagon is bigger and safer."

Linda continued to stare at him, getting angry now. "Bigger, yes, safer, I don't know about," she retorted crisply. "What's gotten into you? You're acting—" She stopped in mid-sentence and turned away from him.

Just that quickly, he sensed her emotional withdrawal from him, and knew that in her mind, at least, he was smothering her. "Overprotective?" He filled in the blank curtly.

She turned back, her glance anything but welcoming as she looked at him. "And then some. I thought we had settled this, the day I put the sign up. I'm perfectly capable of taking care of myself. I don't need you or anyone else telling me what to do or when and how to do it!"

Clearly, she resented his insistence she go home—now. As an independent adult, he couldn't blame her. As her lover, in the face of her willful disregard for her own safety, he was angry. "Is that what you think I'm doing?" he volleyed back.

"Aren't you?"

He fell silent, unable to think of a good answer. "I can see this was a mistake—coming here." But he couldn't just sit home and do nothing, all the while knowing she was in danger.

"You can say that again," Linda grumbled under her breath, moving back to her desk. Sitting down, she again immersed herself in paperwork.

He was stunned when he realized, after all this, she still meant to stay on. His teeth clenched as he watched her pinpoint the next name on her list, reach for the phone and start to dial. "Linda—"

"Ross, if you want to stay my friend, get out of here, now," she warned, twin spots of color appearing in her cheeks.

He knew she was right, that he should leave, that he had no right to tell her what to do or when to do it. She was an adult.

He told himself to head for the door.

But his feet wouldn't budge. They were glued to the floor.

Linda, having had enough, put the phone back down, got up again, her motions weary and exaggerated. She crossed to his side and pointed dramatically to the portal. "The door is that way. If you don't mind, Ross, I have work to do."

Her direction, so loftily given, took him back to another time and place. To a time with a tragic ending. His own temper exploded. Before he could stop himself he had closed the small distance between them with one short step. He glared down at her, aware they were almost nose to nose. "As it happens, I do mind. Very much." Aware it was all he could do not to grab her and shake some sense into her, he continued rigidly, "You may not care what happens to you, but there are over sixty-five kids counting on you to be here tomorrow when they come in. Maybe people can't always choose the time to live or die, but to take stupid, risky chances just for the hell of it has got to be the most selfish, stupid thing a person could do!"

Linda stepped back, her mouth agape. And then without warning, her face changed. She stopped being on the defensive and took the offensive. "Are we talking about me here?" she queried in a cool, clear voice. "Or someone else?" she finished on a clear, bitter note.

It was Ross's turn to be surprised.

Knowing she'd hit a nerve, she stepped closer again. His gaze softened as she searched his eyes for the clues that would explain his emotional state. "This isn't about us. It's about you. Your past. Something that happened. This has something to do with Karen, doesn't it?" she whispered hesitantly at last. "With how she died."

Ross realized she was right. His anxiety came from the past, and it affected the present, even the future. He didn't want a tragedy happening again, not if he could prevent it. He also saw the only way he would ever be able to convince Linda to go home now was if he explained.

"I know she was in a car accident," Linda said. "Was it icy that night, too?"

He wasn't surprised she'd put two and two together. Only that she hadn't done so sooner.

"It was snowing, actually," Ross said. His mind flew back to that terrible time. His voice grew tormented. "Karen never did like driving in the ice or snow, but she was competent at it. Like you are, I guess. Anyway, I always worried whenever she was out behind the wheel during weather like that." Linda was silent, wide-eyed, listening.

"The night she died she had a class at the university. I wanted to take her and pick her up later, but she thought it was silly to take the baby out in that weather, and insisted on driving herself." Ross's hands balled into fists at his side as he continued. "Coming home, she hit a patch of ice and her car spun out of control."

Silence fell between them, painful and bitter, laced with his own regret. "Ross, you can't blame yourself for that!" Linda whispered in an anguished voice.

Ross only wished it were that simple. He turned away from her. "Can't I?" he asked woodenly. "I knew from the outset there was danger. Every instinct in me told me to forbid her to go unless she agreed to let me drive her, but I didn't do that, and because I didn't, she died." God, he still had nightmares about it. Just talking about it dredged up a choking layer of guilt.

Linda stared at Ross. Her chin set stubbornly, she moved around the office agitatedly. When she turned back to him, she looked at him with greatly strained patience. "Yes, and maybe she would've died anyway." He looked up, stunned, and she continued in a steely voice. "If not in a car accident, then from cancer, or a fall in the shower, or something else equally unpredictable and senseless." She moved toward him, tears shimmering in her dark blue eyes.

She held out her hands beseechingly, as she pleaded for him to put the guilt that had been haunting him for two years aside. "Ross, these things happen. No one is to blame. You can think of it as fate, or God's will, or whatever, but I think, to a certain point, that our destiny in life is unavoidable."

Ross had thought that himself once. A very long time ago. One side of his mouth turning up ruefully, he paraphrased, "Or in other words, when your time's up, your time's up."

"Yes." Her gaze was brilliant, compelling and full of understanding.

But Ross found it impossible to be as easy on himself as she was being. Linda hadn't been there. She didn't know how simple it would have been for him to prevent the tragic event.

But dwelling on that mistake wouldn't make it go away, he knew. He was quiet a long moment, wishing he could put his guilt over his wife's death behind him once and for all. "I still think I should have done something to prevent Karen from going to class that night," he said with brutal honesty, "but I didn't." Yes it was over now, and there was nothing he could do about it—except continue to blame himself. If only that could bring some relief, he thought heavily.

Linda moved closer. She gently touched his arm. "You're only responsible for yourself, Ross. And Kimberly, until she grows up and is on her own. No one else."

Looking into her eyes, Ross could almost believe that. Almost. Lord knew he wanted to believe it.

Sensing they'd made all the headway they could on that issue, for now at least, Linda withdrew. "I think you're right," she said, stuffing work into her briefcase. "I better be going home."

He knew now she was doing this for him, not for herself. Ross was silent a moment, watching her. Then he said, "You won't let me drive you?"

Her glance holding his with bewitching intensity, she shook her head. "No. But I am glad you came over tonight. I'm glad you told me about Karen. That was something I needed to know."

She did understand him, even if she didn't approve of his actions. Ross watched as she turned off the lights and started for the door. "I don't suppose I could change your mind," he said, looking wistfully out at the lot where both their cars were parked. Damn, but he wanted to protect her. To shield her from even the possibility of harm.

Rain continued to fall steadily, without a hint yet of sleet or snow. Beside them, the thermometer that hung on the outside of the building still read thirty-four.

"No," she said softly. "You know you can't and you know why."

"Because you're a strong independent woman."

"Right." Impulsively she stood on tiptoe and brushed his cheek with her soft, unglossed lips. The hint of mint on her breath mixed with the subtle aroma of her perfume. "But I thank you for caring," she whispered.

Her tenderness flooded him with sensation. Where her lips had touched his skin, he tingled. The rest of him, heart and soul, ached for longer, closer contact.

Acting equally on impulse, he clasped both her arms and turned her to him. Without waiting to test her response, he let his mouth lower over hers. He kissed her long and hard, putting everything he felt for her in that single kiss. When he released her long moments later, both were trembling slightly, shivering from both the cold of the night and the heat of the kiss, the damp icy wind whipping up around them.

"Thank you," he said softly, holding her close one last time, "for being you." She might be defiant and stubborn sometimes, but she'd brought delight and vivacity back into his life. It was getting so that he didn't know what he would ever do without her. And he prayed he would never have to find out.

Chapter Nine

"Hi, Tad. How are you this morning?"

"Fine, Ms. Harrigan." Tad came up and gave her a quick hug, then hurried off to have first dibs on the classroom's toy and book selection.

"You look great today," Linda remarked to Tad's mother. Wendy, too, was there early, especially for a Wednesday morning, walking in just seconds after the door had opened, which was unusual for Wendy who seemed to run perpetually late.

"I've got an important client coming in today," Wendy confided, straightening the hem of her navy suit jacket. "A relocating executive and his wife. If I make a sale I'll get a full commission on it."

Linda smiled. She could tell this was a big day for Wendy. "Nervous?"

"A little," Wendy admitted. "But I was up half the night going over the listings in the northwest area, so I'm prepared to show the Armstrongs whatever they want to see." She hurried over to Tad, who was already taking a bucket of blocks from the shelf. "'Bye, honey." She bent down to give him a kiss and a hug. "I'll see you tonight."

"'Bye, Mommy." He kissed her back, and then returned his attention to his blocks.

As Wendy left, Dexter came in, followed by Bethany and Laura, then Marylou. The girls all said hi to Tad and, interested in what he was doing, sat down and began to help out. The group played contentedly for about five minutes while Linda began sorting out the materials for their art project.

Appearing to lose interest, Tad surrendered the blocks to the girls and went over to take a book from the shelf. He curled up with it in the corner in a beanbag chair. When Linda looked again, half an hour later, she noticed he was dozing. He also appeared a little flushed. She walked over to him and put her hand on his forehead. He was burning up! Surely Wendy had noticed this when she kissed him goodbye.

Linda called in one of the Center's two circulating teacher aides to take over her class. Taking Tad by the hand, she helped him stand up. "Let's go to my office. I want to take your temperature."

It was one hundred and one. She made him lie down on the sofa, got a pillow and blanket for him, and then called Wendy's office. The secretary said she had no way to reach her. "She'll be out showing houses all day."

"Yes, I know," Linda retorted patiently, "but her son is sick." Surely they could understand this was an emergency.

"I'm sorry, but like I said, there's really nothing I can do until Wendy either calls the office or comes back in to write up a contract. But I promise I'll tell her as soon as she does come in."

"Thank you." Aware of Tad's presence, Linda gently put down the phone.

He looked up at her, his expression hopeful. "Is my Mommy coming?"

"As soon as she can, darling." Unfortunately, in the meantime, Linda couldn't do anything else for him. She had an aspirin substitute on hand, but she had no idea if Wendy had given Tad anything for the fever earlier, and so she couldn't give Tad any medication without getting Wendy's okay first. Fortunately, however, Tad didn't seem sick enough to warrant a visit to a doctor. Right now it looked like the flu.

Assured by the small boy that his stomach felt fine, Linda got him some apple juice. Tad sipped the cool liquid gratefully then lay back down. Soon he was asleep.

Linda spent the morning running back and forth between her office and her classroom. She tried Wendy again at noon. Still no luck. Worried because Tad's temperature had climbed to 103 and he was increasingly lethargic, Linda called Tad's pediatrician. Dr. Isaacs agreed to see Tad on her lunch hour.

Dr. Isaacs pronounced it the flu, gave Tad some acetominophen to bring the fever down, reasoning that enough time had elapsed to allow a second dose even if a first had indeed been given, and prescribed bed rest and isolation until the fever had been gone for twenty-four hours. "Unfortunately," Dr. Isaacs concluded, "This flu bug is very virulent. You'll probably see a lot more of it at your Center before it's over."

Great, Linda thought, just great. She drove Tad back to school and made him comfortable on her sofa once again. The acetominophen helped, and Tad promptly went back to sleep. He awoke later asking for more juice and watched *Sesame Street* and *Mr. Rogers* on the small portable television in Linda's office.

When Wendy came in just before six, Linda had to struggle to keep the anger from her voice. Taking Wendy aside, she explained what had transpired.

Wendy's expression became rueful. "I thought he might be coming down with something this morning."

"But you brought him to school anyway." Knowing this made Linda furious.

Wendy gestured helplessly. "I had this client—"

With effort, Linda kept her voice down. For her, this was the worst aspect of child-care. "Wendy, your child was sick! And now, because of what you did, half the kids in this Center might get sick, too."

"I'm sorry."

Linda's mouth compressed tightly as she expressed her disapproval. "*Sorry* doesn't cut it. If you do it again, I'll have to ask you to place Tad elsewhere. I won't have all the kids here suffering because of the misjudgment of a parent." She paused, letting her words sink in. Swallowing, she made a last-ditch effort to control her temper. "Am I making myself clear?"

Wendy nodded, looking upset and ashamed. "I'm sorry," she said, her eyes misting. "I know I haven't been as attentive to Tad as I should have been the past few months, but I've been under so much pressure with the classes and the exams and my new career!" She burst into guilty tears.

Linda knew Wendy loved her son. And also that financially she had been desperate. This really wasn't like her. From the sincerely apologetic look on her face, Linda could tell Wendy had learned her lesson.

Linda's anger abated somewhat, and she sighed, then asked in a resigned tone, "Did you make the sale?" She hoped she had. It would have been hard to take if this had all been for naught.

Wendy nodded, smiling now through her tears. "I earned three thousand dollars today. That's enough to buy groceries for a year." She looked down at the floor, knowing that was no excuse. "I'm sorry, Linda. I knew Tad was sick this morning. But I . . . I really needed this sale." She choked up again, and couldn't continue. Tears streamed silently down her face.

Seeing her obvious distress, knowing Wendy felt she'd been caught in an impossible situation—one that would force her to lose no matter what path she took, Linda felt a little guilty for giving her such a hard time. She'd never been in Wendy's situation, one where she had to scramble just to get money for food, but she could sympathize. And now that Wendy had a little nest egg to fall back on, she wouldn't be under quite so much pressure in the future. "Just don't let it happen again, okay?" she said softly. "If he is sick, and you have to work, get a sitter or a nurse to come to your home."

"Okay." Their discussion over, Wendy went in to wake Tad, who'd drifted off to sleep on the sofa again. He was happy to see his mother, and all too glad to be going home.

By Friday, Linda's worst fears had materialized. Six more kids were out with the flu, and two more became ill during the day. Ross called to cancel their date for that night. "Kimberly's not feeling well. I'm not sure what it is. Her temperature is only ninety-nine point eight, but..."

"It'll probably go up," Linda predicted with a sigh. "We've been hit with a flu bug here at school, it started Wednesday when one of the kids came to school sick."

"You sent the child home, didn't you?"

Linda saw no sense in upsetting Ross further; he had enough to deal with just caring for Kimberly. She evaded carefully, "Yes, I sent him home as soon as it was possible to do so. I also kept him isolated from the others, but it's a contagious virus."

Ross sighed, accepting the fact that these things happened, no matter how careful one was. "How long does it take to run its course?" he asked, an undertone of worry in his voice.

"The doctor said forty-eight hours, barring complications." And indeed Tad had come back to school that morning, fever-free and looking chipper. She paused. "Is there anything I can do to help?"

"Yes," he joked, "pray I don't get it."

She laughed. "That's easy enough, but seriously, do you think Kimberly might want some chicken soup? I'm not good at cooking that from scratch, but I can run to the store and buy some Campbell's." In fact, she wouldn't mind sitting up with him and Kimberly.

He laughed at her offer, appreciating the spirit in which it had been given. "That's okay, Linda. I've got some." He paused. "Look, why don't you give me a raincheck on tonight? I'll tend to Kimberly. You've got enough on your plate, and I probably wouldn't be very good company anyway. Let's get together as soon as Kimberly is better, okay?"

Linda closed her eyes, remembering the weekend, how it felt to be held and loved by him. "You've got it," she promised softly.

"READ IT AGAIN, Daddy." Kimberly snuggled next to Ross on the sofa. Wrapped in robe and slippers, her light blond hair braided into two shimmering ropes, her eyes shining with excitement, she looked much better than she had that morning when they'd got up.

"Feeling better, I guess?" The evening before, with her fever peaking at 101 degrees, she had been too lethargic to listen to the story even once.

"Much better, Daddy. Maybe I can even go to school on Monday."

"We'll wait and see," Ross said cautiously. "Sorry, kitten, but you have to be clear of fever twenty-four hours before you can go back to school. I'm not promising anything until I see that temp of yours come down all the way."

Kimberly's lower lip thrust forward as she considered that fact with a petulance that was almost comical. "Oh, all right," she said finally. "But can I see Linda this weekend, anyway?"

Ross was glad his daughter was becoming fonder of Linda. So was he, though *fond* was definitely too weak a description. "Yes, you can see Linda. Now where were we?"

Kimberly pointed to the page. "Right here, Daddy. Ernie just made a terrible mess...."

Lifetime Guarantee

Ross GAVE KIMBERLY a final dose of acetominophen and tucked her in at eight-thirty. She snuggled into sleep almost immediately, and exhausted himself he turned in, too.

He awoke shortly after midnight. Kimberly was standing at the foot of his bed. She was dressed in her pajama top and part of a princess costume she'd worn for Halloween. Her hands were on her hips, and her manner was aggressive and unpleasant. "Where's my costume, Daddy?" she demanded.

Ross sat up blinking, turned on the light. "What?" he repeated, confused but more awake. Kimberly looked strange, not herself.

"Where's my costume, Daddy? I want to go trick-or-treating!"

Ross stared at her, exasperated and amused. She must be dreaming, he thought. Walking in her sleep. Though she'd never done it before, there was a first time for everything. "Honey, it's November," he explained patiently. "Halloween is over. Don't you remember we already went trick-or-treating?"

"Stop teasing me, Daddy!" Kimberly stomped her foot with uncharacteristic belligerence. "I want to go trick-or-treating!"

Ross got out of bed and reached for his robe. Belting it, he walked over and crouched down to her level. Hands on her shoulders, he shook her gently. "Kimberly, honey, you're dreaming. Wake up."

To his stunned amazement, Kimberly recoiled violently from his touch and moved to a corner of the room. She looked frightened and confused. "Don't give me any broccoli!" she said, beginning to cry. "I hate broccoli!"

"Broccoli?" Ross repeated, confused. Crossing to his daughter, despite her efforts to elude him, he gathered her up into his arms. Immediately he realized what the problem was. She was burning up with fever again, and she must be hallucinating. Holding her tightly, he carried her to the stairs, and in a panic, shouted for help. "Mrs. Delancey! Come quick!"

THE TRIP TO THE HOSPITAL was a nightmare. Kimberly cried and resisted being put in the car, but once they were on the way, she became almost too quiet and subdued. His heart pounding in fear, Ross rushed her into the emergency room. Their family doctor, whom Mrs. Delancey had called, was there, and within minutes, Kimberly was being examined.

Ross stayed with her throughout the ordeal while Mrs. Delancey went to call Linda. When she got there, the worst was over. Kimberly had already been through blood tests, a lumbar puncture, an electroencephalogram, and skull X ray, and had been admitted to the pediatric ICU.

"It's Reye's syndrome," Ross said.

Linda stared at him in disbelief. "But how?" she asked. Not Kimberly. Not lovely, sweet Kimberly.

"I don't know," Ross whispered, struggling to keep his voice normal. They were standing outside his daughter's room, keeping watch over her through the glass. The doctors had sedated her, to keep her quiet and hence decrease the blood flow and pressure to the brain. She appeared to be resting comfortably, no longer upset by her surroundings.

Ross continued, agitated and upset, obviously blaming himself. "I didn't give her aspirin. Don't even have any in the house. Only acetaminophen." He buried his head in his hands.

"Is she going to be all right?"

Numbly he repeated what the doctor had said: "Only time will tell." He swallowed hard. "For now we just have to wait."

"DID I EVER TELL YOU about the night Kimberly was born?" Ross asked softly from his chair at his daughter's bedside. It was late on Sunday night. Kimberly had been in the hospital almost twenty-four hours. Linda had stayed with him throughout the ordeal, holding his hand, just being there for him. She was as frightened for his daughter as he was, but for his sake, she tried not to show it. Instead she kept up a cheery front that promised everything would be fine, given time and the expertise of the doctors.

"No." She handed him the coffee she'd bought from the machine.

Ross was unshaven and exhausted. Kimberly was sleeping peacefully, looking, except for the tubes running into her arms and the complicated lifesaving apparatus surrounding her, like a sleeping princess just waiting to be magically awakened.

He took a sip. His eyes remained on his daughter as he recounted, "Karen was exhausted after the delivery and she was asleep. Kimberly was wide awake. The nurses brought her to me and let me hold her." He smiled. "She was just so perfect then, so pretty and tiny. She only weighed six pounds. But I loved her then, from the first moment she looked up at me." He forced himself to take another swallow of the bitter black brew as his eyes filled with tears, then said, his voice wavering emotionally, "I think she knew who I was even then." His shoulders trembled in helpless agony as the moisture slid down his face. Linda crossed silently to his side and slipped her arms around him.

"She's going to be all right," Linda said fiercely, silently willing it to be true.

"I hope so," Ross whispered, leaning against her. "I really hope so."

By Monday morning there was no change. Kimberly hadn't gotten any worse, but she hadn't gotten measurably better, either. Ross had dozed off for a time in the early hours of the morning, and Linda had gone to his house to get him a fresh change of clothes. With the nurse's permission, he'd used a shower there at the hospital around dawn. Newly shaved, he looked tired, but refreshed. And still he kept his vigil over his tiny daughter.

"It's amazing how small she looks in this bed," Ross murmured. Kimberly was lying in a stainless-steel crib, the sides partially raised to keep her from tumbling out. "At four, I think she's so big and yet she's really so small."

Too small to be going through this, Linda thought.

And again she silently willed the doctor's efforts to work. She prayed that Kimberly would get better and emerge unscathed.

Ross continued to watch his daughter in silent contemplation.

When he spoke, his voice was low, self-condemning. "I keep thinking about all the times I was too busy. Too short-tempered. Too self-involved."

"Ross, I can't believe..." She'd seen what a good father he was. No one could have asked for more.

"I always wanted to be the perfect father."

"No one can be that," Linda said fiercely, feeling tears well up in her eyes. She blinked them back.

"Maybe I should have tried harder." He moved away from the crib and spoke in a low voice only Linda could hear. "Maybe I'm being punished."

"No! You've done everything you could." She reached for him and held him close. "You've got to get some rest. She's going to need you when she feels better."

He held her tighter. "When she gets better," Ross murmured.

"Yes," Linda said, "yes..."

UNFORTUNATELY, there were no quick solutions, no easy medical cures. The next few days were a nightmare of waiting, watching. Kimberly was fed intravenously and attended by private nurses around the clock.

Slowly, day by day, she grew stronger. When the doctor told them Wednesday that she was going to be all right, Ross and Linda both burst into tears of happiness and relief.

By Friday, Kimberly was out of the intensive-care unit, off the intravenous, sitting up in bed, demanding ice cream and stories. Yet despite the improvement in her condition, Ross continued to hover over her, watching for any little sign she might worsen again. Linda understood. She knew only too well how close he had come to losing his daughter. Yet she wondered, too, if he shouldn't begin to recover from the ordeal. To relax and accept the fact his daughter really was going to be okay.

"I want Linda to read a story to me this time, Daddy," Kimberly decided.

Linda smiled as Ross appeared miffed. "Hey! I'm the daddy!" He pretended to be hurt.

"I know, but Linda reads good, too," Kimberly said seriously. She tilted her head sideways, teasing him now. "Please, Daddy? You can read the next one."

Ross laughed at her comical expression. "All right," he said finally. "I bow to the real teacher here."

Linda drew up a chair next to the bed.

"No," Kimberly said, before Linda could even get the storybook open. She patted the bed beside her. "Up here." Surprised, Linda exchanged a look with Ross and then complied, lowering the side rail. She had known Ross's daughter had gotten gradually closer to her. But this degree of affection and acceptance she hadn't expected, especially after what Kimberly had just been through.

Kimberly snuggled closer. "I want you to put your arm around me, like Daddy does." Again, Linda did as she was bid. She smiled down at Kimberly affectionately, glad to see the little girl had gotten her spirit back. "Anything else?"

Kimberly shook her head and relaxed against Linda in blissful contentment. Then smiled impishly as the next thought struck. "Unless Daddy wants to sit up here on the bed, too."

He looked like he'd been dying to be asked. Linda would've laughed had she not experienced firsthand his anguish the past few days. Surely he would stop hovering so anxiously over Kimberly in another day or two, wouldn't he? As it was, he could barely be persuaded to leave his daughter's room, even for a minute. It was almost as if he didn't trust her to be out of his sight, out of his circle of protection. And Linda knew that would be unhealthy, if it continued.

"I don't know," said Ross, already moving around the bed and lowering the rail on the other side. "Will this bed take all the weight?"

"I think so." Linda smiled. She was being silly, worrying too much! Of course Ross was still anxious. He'd been through an ordeal, and at least one good thing had come out of it. The three of them were almost like a real family. Who would have guessed the trauma of Kimberly's illness would bring them together?

She wouldn't trade this newfound closeness for the world. Not for anything.

"WHEN IS KIMBERLY coming back to school?" Linda asked the following Friday. She was at Ross's, drying dishes, after a late-night supper for just the two of them. Mrs. Delancey was off, touring San Antonio. Kimberly was upstairs fast asleep.

"I don't know yet." He frowned, as if it weren't something he really wanted to discuss.

Linda studied him carefully. "What'd the doctor say?" She was aware Kimberly had gone to see Dr. Isaacs the day before.

"That she can go back anytime now, next Monday if she wants." He paid particular attention to scrubbing the Crockpot in his hands.

Ah, now they were getting somewhere, she mused. Linda had seen this syndrome before. "But you don't want her to?" she guessed gently.

Ross paused. "He told me that anytime you get a room full of preschoolers together, there's illness. That it's unavoidable no matter what precautions you take."

Linda put down her dishtowel and sought to reassure him. "Did her doctor also tell you that the children eventually develop immunities because they're exposed to the different viruses, and that they also face exposure to illness every time they leave their house, go to the grocery store, church, the movie theater?" Ross was an intelligent man. He had to see there was no way he could shelter Kimberly indefinitely, no matter how much he tried.

"Yeah, he mentioned that, too," Ross admitted quietly, the look on his face telling her that although he might have bought that theory intellectually, he couldn't accept it emotionally.

"But you still want to keep her out," Linda prompted, thinking that Ross had to get his feelings about this out in the open where he could explore them, discover how irrational they were. Granted, it was understandable he would react this way, but that still didn't make it the best situation for Kimberly.

He turned to her, wanting her to understand. "Linda, she's been through so much. I just...don't want her getting sick again." He finished on a stubborn note.

Linda repressed a sigh. "And you're afraid if she does come back to school..."

His eyes narrowed. "You know it's possible. Especially in the winter months, when there are outbreaks of strep throat and bronchitis..." His voice trailed off, as he brooded about the worst.

"Well, maybe you're right," Linda said, finishing the last dish. She hung up her towel to dry and leaned against the counter to face Ross. "Maybe it wouldn't hurt to keep her home a few more days, but as for much longer, well, you realize the Thanksgiving pageant and feast are scheduled for next Wednesday. If she doesn't come back she'll have to miss both and you know how important it is to her. The kids have been working toward it for weeks now."

"I know. If she seems fine, if there's no other illness at school, she'll probably be able to go."

Just probably. Linda started to question him, then stopped herself. She had to be understanding. Ross had come close to losing his daughter. It was natural he'd want to hold on tight. She'd give him a few more days, time to cool down, see reason.

She closed the distance between them and put her arms around him. He held her tight. "Promise me you won't wait too long," she murmured. Kimberly needed contact with her peers. If she didn't have it, she would slip back into a state of excessive shyness again. Linda didn't want to see Kimberly forfeit all the ground she had gained.

He slid a finger under her chin and tipped her face up to his. "I promise," he murmured huskily, changing the subject completely. And she realized that she wasn't the only one with another subject on her mind.

Chapter Ten

"Linda, please don't go to work," Kimberly said tearfully Tuesday morning as Linda prepared to leave. "Stay here with me."

Linda bent down to face her at eye level. "Honey, I can't. I have to teach." She had dropped by after breakfast to give Kimberly some school assignments. None were really crucial; they were mostly color-cut-and-paste projects, a few basic worksheets on letters of the alphabet, and the stories she'd read to the class while Kimberly had been away.

As Linda had expected, Kimberly was delighted to do the work. Now that she was better, she was getting bored hanging around the house all day. Unfortunately for Kimberly, Ross had adamantly refused to let her go back to school just yet. Thinking he was bound to come around soon, Linda hadn't pushed him. Now, looking at Kimberly's miserable expression, she wondered if she'd been wise.

"Then take me with you," Kimberly pleaded, wrapping her arms tightly around Linda's neck. "Please. I want to see my friends! I want to be in the

Thanksgiving pageant! I want to rehearse with the other kids!"

Linda frowned, thinking. Kimberly had a point. The pageant and feast were tomorrow evening. And Kimberly had missed almost every runthrough of the staged activities. She looked at Mrs. Delancey. Mrs. Delancey lifted her shoulders helplessly, mouthing, "I don't know what to do, either."

"Please take me with you," Kimberly said again, moving back slightly and turning on the full powers of her persuasive charm. "I'm better now. All better. Even Daddy says so!"

But what Ross hadn't said was that Kimberly could go back to school today, Linda thought worriedly. Instead, he'd said vaguely, "Maybe...tomorrow." And as close as she was to the family, she couldn't do anything without Ross's permission. "Well, let me call your dad and see what he says," she said finally, hoping she could persuade Ross to let Kimberly go in at least for today.

Then, maybe if Kimberly weathered one day without incident, Ross would see his way clear to let her weather the next and the next. Heaven knew, if Kimberly didn't get back in school she would lose all the ground she had gained.

Unfortunately Ross wasn't in yet when Linda phoned his office. And she was already running late.

Kimberly continued to be tearfully insistent. Caught between a rock and a hard place, Linda decided finally to go with her gut instinct and do what was right for the child. She was fairly sure Ross would be furious with her, and also fairly sure she could charm her way out of the sticky situation. In fact, it would probably be a cinch once Ross saw how happy Kimberly was. And this way he wouldn't have to worry, wondering if she was all right during those first few hours.

She turned to Mrs. Delancey. "I'll take responsibility for this. She'll be fine."

Mrs. Delancey nodded, looking relieved. Apparently she agreed with Linda that Kimberly belonged back in preschool, especially since the child wanted so badly to return.

To Linda's delight, Kimberly was welcomed back to her class with open arms. Her classmates were ecstatic to see her again, and the whole morning passed quickly, with everyone getting along splendidly. The pageant rehearsal went well, the noon meal similarly pleasant. When rest period came, Kimberly and the others fell quickly into an exhausted sleep on their cots. With the parent volunteers watching over the class, Linda returned to her office. It was then that Ross came storming in, his face a thundercloud. "What the hell do you think you're doing, dragging her down here?" he demanded, sotto voce, the moment the door was closed.

Linda caught her breath. Maybe this wasn't going to be as easy as she'd thought. "You are so damn irresponsible at times!" he continued furiously, not giving her a chance to answer.

His scathing assessment stung, but Linda told herself it was his emotions talking now, not his intellect, and he didn't mean half of what he was saying. At least he wouldn't when he had the chance to stop and think about it. Drawing on all the self-control she possessed, Linda said, "She's fine, Ross. And she had a wonderful time this morning. You should have seen her rehearsing for the pageant."

At the mention of the pageant, his face darkened even more. "That's not the point and you know it!"

The last of her self-control snapped. Linda jumped to her feet. "You're right. That's not the point. The point is you're smothering her with protectiveness, and it's got to stop!" she whispered back vehemently. Both hands splayed across the top of her desk, Linda fought for calm. In a quieter, albeit emotional, voice she explained, "I love you, I love her." To her dismay, Ross remained stonily distant. "I'm only trying to help. She was so unhappy this morning, Ross, literally begging to go to school with me. It almost broke my heart. And if you don't believe me, you can ask Mrs. Delancey."

"I already did," he snapped back. "But that doesn't change anything. The fact of the matter is I did not give Kimberly permission to go back to school."

And he wasn't about to forgive Linda for expediting the matter. "I'm going to get her now and take her home. We can talk about this later."

"Ross, she's asleep—" Linda said, starting after him.

"With any luck at all, then, she won't wake up."

But of course, Kimberly did wake up, as did several others. Groggy and disoriented, she resisted her father's efforts to put on her coat and shoes. Linda said goodbye gently, then looked up at Ross. He was still furious.

But their argument would have to wait. She had a class to teach.

The rest of the afternoon was a disaster. The children were grumpy and argumentative, because none had really had enough of a nap. Linda was distracted and upset.

By the time she reached Ross's home at seven that evening, she was even more strung out. One look at his grim face told her he hadn't relented in the slightest. She sighed, not sure where to begin.

"Linda, hi!" Kimberly ran into the entry hall, already clad in her pajamas. She had an apron wrapped around her middle and was waving a wooden spoon. If she was the worse for wear after her three-quarters of a day at school, Linda thought wryly, she couldn't see it.

"I'm going to make apple crisp!" Kimberly continued excitedly. "Mrs. Delancey was going to help me, but now you can! It's for the pageant!"

"The pageant," Ross repeated, dumbstruck. He turned to stare at his daughter. Obviously, this was something they hadn't discussed.

"Don't you remember, Daddy?" Kimberly's face twisted into an impatient scowl. "Linda said we had to bring apple crisp to the Thanksgiving feast. Tad is bringing mashed potatoes. Bethany is bringing corn—"

"Oh, yes." Ross finally caught up with her. "Well, I meant to talk to you about that," he said reluctantly, looking at his daughter. To Linda, "We can still bring the food we were slated to bring, of course, but—" Ross turned back to Kimberly "—I don't think you're going to go, honey. You're just not well enough yet."

Linda's jaw dropped open. Kimberly looked aghast. "Daddy!" she cried.

Ross swallowed so hard his Adam's apple bobbed up and down. "It's going to be a late night, a lot of people. It's just...soon for you to be going back, honey. I'm sorry. Maybe next year..."

As he spoke, big tears rolled down Kimberly's face. Her chin quivered as she studied his stern expression. "But Daddy—"

"Ross, please, it's only one night," Linda intervened.

Ross sent Linda a fierce glance, silently instructing her to stay out of it. With a reassuring smile, he turned back to his daughter. "Kimberly, go upstairs. I'll come up and talk to you soon."

Mrs. Delancey came out of the kitchen in time to hear the last. She looked at Ross as though he was a criminal, then reached for Kimberly's hand. "Come on, darling. I'll read you a story. Maybe even two."

Kimberly wasn't appeased. Still crying, she let Mrs. Delancey lead her toward the stairs. Halfway up, she turned and begged, "Make my daddy change his mind, Linda. Please."

"Come on, Kimberly," Mrs. Delancey urged. They disappeared out of sight.

Linda turned back to Ross, her own emotions running very high. "I can't believe you did that to her," she accused tonelessly.

Ross's expression grew stony with the depth of his resolve. And she saw then what an iron grip the past— and his fear of losing someone he loved again—still had on him. "I ignored my instincts about danger once," he said flatly. "I won't do it again."

Linda stood perfectly still for a moment. His house was warm, but a shiver ran through her. She crossed her arms and held them tight against her waist.

He shook his head miserably. "Everything inside me tells me it's too soon for her to be going back to school," he continued gruffly, his green eyes defensive, "that she's just not strong enough yet."

Linda watched him rake a hand through his cornsilk hair. If it had been just himself he was hurting, it would have been one thing, but he was hurting his daughter too. And that she wouldn't stand by and watch.

"She's not strong enough, or you're not strong enough, Ross?" Linda probed coldly, in an effort to get through to him. She continued, angry that his fear had made him blind to the consequences of his actions. "It seems to me Kimberly is coping just fine. You're the one who can't handle the stress." And it was wrong for him to penalize his daughter for his own shortcomings, she thought.

But her advice was falling on deaf ears. "Linda, you are butting in where you don't belong," he warned.

"Ross, you're being cruel!"

He reeled back, as if he'd just sustained a blow to the jaw. His face changed. He delivered the next punch with lethal accuracy, "And you're being careless with my daughter's life!"

Linda was stung. If he really thought that, he didn't know her at all. "I love Kimberly," she declared passionately.

"But not enough. Otherwise you'd be helping me to protect her from further illness, trying to keep her from further danger." He advanced on Linda emotionally. "Are you forgetting that just two weeks ago she was in intensive care?"

No, Linda hadn't. Nor had she chosen to ignore the fact that Kimberly was fully recovered now. "There's no such thing as absolute safety, Ross," she pointed out calmly. "You and I both know that. No matter how much you try to protect her, she could still get strep throat tomorrow!"

"But there are such things as precautionary measures." He muttered an oath, threw up his hands and wheeled away from her. "Why is it so hard for you to understand? After all she's just been through, I don't want her getting sick again!"

That's what he was telling himself, but it just wasn't true. "No, you just don't want to let go," Linda corrected. Why couldn't he see what he was doing? "You're smothering her." Just as she had been smothered.

"Now who's casting stones?" Ross retorted.

Linda had no answer for that. She knew it wasn't true, but realized she'd never convince him of that, not the way he was feeling now. She said nothing in response. The uneasy silence continued. Ross refused to give an inch.

Tears filled Linda's eyes as her thoughts returned to Kimberly and how all this quarreling was bound to affect her. Not to mention what Ross was doing in depriving Kimberly of the chance to be in the Thanksgiving pageant. "I can't stand by and watch you do this to your daughter," she said hoarsely. She loved the both of them too much to stoically endure their hurt, especially when it could all be fixed so easily with just one word of permission on Ross's part.

He looked as if he felt similarly betrayed. "Then don't," Ross snapped.

Linda flinched and watched his expression grow bitter. "You're only making things worse. For Kimberly and for me. If you'd just support me in this, Kimberly would get over missing the pageant."

But Linda knew it wouldn't get easier for Ross to put Kimberly back in school, only harder. With every day that passed, Ross's fears grew larger; unless he confronted them now, openly and honestly, he would never be able to do so. "If you think that, then you're a fool," she asserted quietly. Blinking back new tears, she said, "These programs and performances mean everything to the kids. They work very hard to set them up, to ensure their success. It can be a very special time for the parents and children." Kimberly wasn't the only one who would miss out. Ross would lose, too.

Ross's jaw hardened. "Then I guess I am a fool," he shot back acerbically. "Because I really thought, having you there with me when Kimberly was sick, that you would understand firsthand what I'm going through now and back me on this. I thought you'd make an effort to accept my decision, despite how disappointed she is." His eyes darkened passionately and his voice dropped another husky notch. "And I'm a fool, because I really thought a relationship between us could work."

Linda's voice caught and wavered. "So did I." But she could see now the idea was ludicrous. They were too different after all. A life together would be a constant battle, with Kimberly in the middle. "It's over, isn't it?" she whispered hoarsely, wishing she felt more than this awful numbness, this raw, aching disbelief.

"It has to be," Ross said, pained. His look of hurt faded, to be replaced by one of challenge, as he threw down the last and final gauntlet. "Unless you change your mind and stand with me on this."

She couldn't do that.

He wouldn't relent, either.

Suddenly there was nothing left to say, nothing left to do, nothing left to salvage. Her tears blinding her, she walked away from him and out the front door. With every step, she half expected him to call her name or come after her. But he didn't. And with her heart feeling like it was broken into a million fragments, Linda got in her car and drove away.

"WHERE'S KIMBERLY? Isn't she coming?" Tad asked Linda the following evening. "I thought she was going to be a lady pilgrim! She knew her lines and everything!" The backstage area was filled with a score of tiny Indians and Pilgrims. Through the closed curtains, they could hear the murmur of the audience waiting for the pageant to begin.

Linda had hoped so, too. But a quick call moments earlier to Mrs. Delancey had confirmed the worst. Ross hadn't changed his mind. And though Kimberly had begged and pleaded with him, he wouldn't back down.

Nevertheless Linda kept thinking Ross might show up. But as the curtain time neared four minutes, then three, then two, she finally had to admit that he wasn't coming.

"No, Tad, she isn't coming," Linda said, trying hard to keep the overwhelming sadness she felt out of her voice.

Dexter came up in his Indian costume. "I wish Kimberly was here, too!"

"So do I," chimed in Laura.

"Me, too," said Linda. But there was nothing more to be done. And the show had to go on.

Happily, the play was a success. The children remembered most of their lines and enacted the first Thanksgiving well, starting with the Pilgrims' voyage across the ocean, then the settling of the new land, the negotiating with the Indians, and sharing the first Thanksgiving meal. The parents were thrilled and touched by their children's performances, and so, the feast that followed was a joyous affair.

Still, it was a hollow victory for Linda without Ross and Kimberly. She compensated the only way she knew how—by moving constantly among the parents and staff.

Glenna wasn't fooled by Linda's excessively cheerful facade. "You're devastated, aren't you, that Ross and Kimberly aren't here?" she said later as the two of them cleaned up the buffet.

All the families had left. Only the staff and their spouses remained. "I can't help it," Linda admitted, unable to shake the numbness that pervaded her. Her eyes filled with tears as she thought of the loss both had endured tonight, all because of Ross's stupidly overprotective behavior. "We both worked so hard to expand the preschool. He should be here, sharing in this. So should Kimberly."

Glenna was silent a moment. Then she said consolingly, "Maybe he'll come around, you know, in another month or two, when he gets over almost losing Kimberly."

Linda swallowed around the lump in her throat. If only she could believe that. But she'd seen the look on Ross's face when he'd refused to let Kimberly perform in the pageant. Beneath the stony resolve was a deep fear. He hadn't let go of the fear he'd felt in the hospital, when Kimberly was in the intensive care unit; he might never be able to do so. Maybe if he hadn't lost his wife, so tragically and suddenly, he'd have been able to cope. But he had. And now he was doubly afraid of personal loss. To the point where his fear was crippling them all, impeding their healing. "I don't think so," she said slowly.

Glenna looked crushed. She had obviously expected Linda to promise eventual success. "It's really over?"

It had to be, Linda thought. With the two of them feeling the way they did, there was just no way for them to come together.

Chapter Eleven

Ross kept thinking Kimberly would get over her disappointment at missing the preschool's Thanksgiving celebration. Instead she sank deeper and deeper into depression. Nothing cheered her up. Not their own Thanksgiving dinner, the start of their annual Christmas preparations, a visit to Santa at the mall, or the prospect of a long-awaited visit from his folks. She wouldn't talk to him, wouldn't look at him, and when she did it was as if he'd taken her life away.

After nearly a week of her silence, he decided to take time off work and confront the issue head-on. Right after breakfast, he sat down with her in the living room. Although it was only nine o'clock, she had her crayons and construction paper out and was hard at work. "How long are you going to go on pouting?" Ross asked.

"I'm not pouting," Kimberly said seriously. "I'm sad and lonely." Illustrating her point, she drew a big circle, dotted in two eyes and then a mouth that curved dramatically down.

She'd learned to identify and talk about emotions at preschool, Ross recollected vaguely. Then it had seemed cute. Now it made him vaguely uncomfortable, as if he were to blame. *But I'm not to blame,* Ross thought, *I'm only protecting her.* He was keeping her safe and well, away from the hospital, and all the tests and the needles and the pain.

She could have died from Reye's syndrome, his heart cried.

But she didn't, the logical side of him answered.

He knew now they both had to go on again, full speed ahead. But they had to do it differently, in a way both could live with. And right now the route he'd chosen for Kimberly wasn't working for her. He had to admit that, whether he wanted to or not.

"I'm really lonely," Kimberly continued in the same dull monotone, drawing yet another sad face to go with the first. "I miss my friends."

Maybe it wouldn't be too risky to expose her to one child or two at a time, and his or her germs, Ross thought. Maybe that was the way to go. "Bethany and Laura can come visit here—" he suggested brightly.

His daughter refused to let him finish. She shook her head and put one elbow on the table. "It's not the same," she reported glumly, resting her forehead on her upraised hand. "Besides, Daddy, I want to play on the playground. You know, the one at school?"

It was all Ross could do not to sigh. The tenacity and inner strength Kimberly was exhibiting reminded him of Linda when she had set her mind on something. Pushing the unwelcome thought away, and the multitude of memories it generated—some happy, some painful—he assured his daughter gently, "That can be arranged, you know." He was still a partner in the preschool, still had a key. He could get in anytime.

"Now?" Kimberly jumped up, excitement lighting her face.

Ross tensed, thinking about all those kids, all those germs. It was still flu season. What if she got Reye's syndrome again? What if she got something worse? No, he couldn't risk it. He just couldn't. He'd lost Karen, and now Linda; not Kimberly, too. "When the other kids are gone for the day," he qualified gently. Even if he wanted to take Kimberly there now, he couldn't; not when school was in session. It would be disruptive.

"Oh." Kimberly sat back down and picked up her crayon. She turned it end over end in her hand. The corners of her mouth dropped. "Never mind then, Daddy," she said so softly he could barely hear her. "I don't want to go then. It won't be fun without my friends."

Ross sighed. She wasn't making this any easier on him. Not that he could really blame her, if he tried to look at it from her limited perspective. "Kimberly—" he began placatingly.

But she wasn't listening to him. Her lower lip jutting angrily, Kimberly refused to look at him. "I'm busy now, Daddy," she instructed him in a dull monotone. "I need to finish my coloring first."

Ross sighed, and continued to watch her draw. As the picture took shape, he saw swings and trees. The kids in her picture were all playing in what he supposed was the preschool yard. All of the crudely drawn figures had happy faces. And then, on another sheet of paper, Kimberly drew yet another picture. It was a girl, unhappy and alone, with only the TV for company. Was that how she saw herself? he wondered, suddenly feeling like he'd been dealt a hammer blow to his chest. Was that how she felt? Was that what he wanted for her? And if so, what had he done? What had he done?

"DEXTER, THAT'S WONDERFUL!" Linda exclaimed, studying the answers the gifted three-year-old had typed on the computer screen. "I can't believe how fast you've mastered the new *Monster Math Addition* software. If you keep this up, pretty soon you're going to be ready for subtraction, too!"

Dexter grinned, reveling in the praise. "I like computers," he said shyly.

Linda nodded approvingly. "I know you do."

A moment later, Glenna caught up with Linda on the other side of the lab. She, too, was looking fit and happy these days, as if marriage to Martin were the best thing that could ever have happened to her. Linda wished she had been able to work out her problems with Ross the way Glenna had worked out her problems with Martin. But their situations weren't the same, she counseled herself firmly, trying not to be too depressed. Martin and Glenna had merely experienced some growing pains, whereas she and Ross had fundamental differences. Differences that couldn't be fixed. Still, she missed him, more than she could say. And she wasn't sure she would ever get over that. They'd come so close to being a family....

But she also knew there was no fixing something Ross wouldn't admit was broken. He felt all the repair needed to be done on her side.

Linda admitted at first she'd felt the reverse about him. But lately, as she got more and more distance from the argument, she began to see that they were both wrong, and right.

If only Ross could see that, she thought.

But he didn't. If he did, he would've put Kimberly back in school by now. He would've called or come to see her. He would've put Kimberly in the Thanksgiving pageant, and let all three of them share the sweet specialness of that magical night.

But he hadn't wanted to be part of that night, she realized on a fresh wave of hurt. Instead, he had just walked away. And any day now she expected a visit from his lawyer, sent to put into play those dissolution agreement papers Ross had insisted she sign at the very beginning.

And she really dreaded that. Because if that happened, it would mean the last link between them would be severed. It would mean she would never have reason to see him or Kimberly again. And despite all the friction that had occurred between them, Linda found that thought excruciatingly painful.

"It's amazing, isn't it," Glenna murmured, "how much Dexter's behavior has improved since we identified him as gifted?"

Linda nodded, though to her it was no mystery. They kept him busy all the time, his mind occupied; he had no chance to get into trouble.

"In fact everyone seems to have settled in nicely," Glenna remarked, giving the lab another satisfied glance.

Linda agreed. Even Tad had straightened out and stopped bullying the other children, mostly because he was now getting the attention from his mother that he craved. He no longer had the anger and resentment simmering inside of him. Wendy, too, had recently turned over a new leaf. Shaken by her son's illness, and her own unprecedented reckless disregard for his health, Wendy cut back on her work hours. In turn, she looked happier and more relaxed, too.

In fact, Linda thought, almost everyone was happier these days except herself. Most of that, of course, was due to the breakup with Ross. It seemed she couldn't look anywhere without being reminded of Ross. Before she knew it, she'd be remembering with bittersweet clarity the first time they made love, and then the second. Or thinking of the icy night Ross had stormed down to the Center to "rescue" her. Or remembering how hard and long the two of them had worked on the scenery for the Thanksgiving pageant.

But Linda supposed there was no going back.

Shaking off the low mood, she left the lab and walked back out into the hall. And it was then that she saw Ross walking into the school.

He was casually dressed, in a plaid sport shirt, navy V-neck sweater and tan slacks. He had a tentative half smile on his face, but his eyes, when they met hers, were serious. Almost too serious.

She shifted uneasily. Without warning, her knees began shaking and she had a lump the size of a walnut in her throat. He looked so good, she thought, so handsome and strong. And aloof and alone.

For one brief moment, she let herself hope he might be there to reconcile, but she knew the hope was sheer folly. She was seeing what she wanted to be there on his face, rather than what *was* there—a mixture of calm and uncertainty.

He had always liked things neat and tidy, she remembered miserably. He probably wanted to end their partnership, now that Kimberly was no longer in the school. If that were the case, she told herself it was for the best.

Her spine stiffened as she braced herself for the inevitable. He slammed his hands into the pockets of his pants. His eyes were full of pain, his mouth turning down unhappily. "Can we talk—alone?" he asked simply. "I have something I need to discuss with you."

And she bet she knew what that something was. The dissolution agreement.

Well, Linda thought, even if Ross demanded all his money back, she could probably go to her parents and get a loan and hence keep the expanded school going.

Alone.

"Linda?" he said softly, jerking her back to the present.

At his unexpected nearness, the wellspring of emotion she'd kept pent up surged in her, her heart hammering in her chest. Deciding she would get through this if it killed her, she forced herself to appear calm. "Sure," she said, somehow managing a brief tremulous smile. Just because they were no longer lovers and about to end their partnership didn't mean they couldn't be civil to one another. She could be civil to anyone. She gave him another too bright smile. "We can use my office."

Glancing in her classroom window as she passed, Linda noted her aide had the group well in hand. She led Ross into her office and shut the door.

"I'm here about Kimberly," Ross began without preamble the moment they were alone. "She's unhappy."

Linda stared at him in silence. This was unexpected, but not really the kind of victory she wanted. She hadn't wanted to be right. She'd wanted the conflict between them to end.

"She wants to come back," Ross continued in a resigned tone.

Linda was surprised Ross would tell her this. "And?"

He shrugged, indicating he'd come to grips with the risks and his potential loss as best he could. His eyes held hers for a long moment. "I said it's okay, if that's what she wants. If you'll take her." The words rushed out, stark and unadorned.

Stunned, Linda took a closer look at Ross. He had suffered. Maybe as much as she had. Without warning the heavens opened up again, and her world was suffused with light. Hope. And the traces of the powerful love that had blazed between them. Linda's eyes flooded with tears as she tried to answer him. An onslaught of emotion clogged her throat to the point where she could barely speak. "There's always a place for Kimberly here. You know that."

His eyes held hers, lingered, caressed. "Thanks." His voice sounded scratchy. His gaze never leaving hers, he cleared his throat. "Is tomorrow too soon?"

She shook her head, too overcome with emotion to speak. She could admit the truth to herself now. She had missed Kimberly terribly the past week, and her father even more. Despite his flaws, she loved Ross more than she could say and always would. "I'll look forward to seeing her then."

Ross nodded. Suddenly he looked as if he didn't know what else to say. The ache inside her cut like a knife, and Linda glanced down at her watch. It was too painful to be alone with him this way, too awkward and emotionally wounding after all they had shared. "If that's everything..." she said, wishing she could shake this unceasing sense of vulnerability, the same vulnerability she felt whenever she was around him.

"It's not," Ross said softly. She lifted her head and saw the heartfelt apology in his eyes. Sunshine filled her soul as she began to realize that all was not lost, after all. She let her breath out in a rush.

"I'm sorry. I was wrong," he continued emotionally. "You were right. I was overprotecting Kimberly, just the way I tried to overprotect you." He swallowed hard and closed the gap between them, his fingers closing tightly over hers. "I only hope it's not too late to rectify it."

A week ago, Linda would have said that it was too late. She wouldn't have dared risk her heart again, not to Ross. But a week without him had taught her a lot. It had showed her how lonely her life was without him, how much she needed him and his daughter.

Looking at Glenna, realizing how she had worked through her problems with Martin, had also made an impact on Linda. It had reminded her that no two people were perfect, and that every relationship required work. But if two people really loved one another, the results were well worth the effort.

Her other hand slid into his as she answered gently, her eyes still locked on his, "I know that you did and said those things because you were confused. It was such a shock for both of us when Kimberly was taken ill. All those days she spent in intensive care, with you watching over her. I should have realized how exhausted you were. Trauma like what you and Kimberly went through is not easy to get over."

"So you do understand that now," he said, taking her into his arms.

Linda nodded and leaned against him. "I realize it's okay to get protection from another," she said, basking in the warmth of his body next to hers, "that if it's not stifling it can be good, nourishing even. It's important to be able to let go, too, when it's in the other's interest," she finished fiercely.

Ross slid a hand under her chin and tilted her face up to his. "I have to be honest with you. I can't promise I'll always be able to control my overprotective urges. I've gone through too much pain. But I will try very hard to rein in. If you let me know when I'm doing it, I'll take time out to try to consider things more logically and less emotionally."

Linda could see how much he had grown, if he was able to make such a promise. Maybe it was time she did some compromising, too. She moved away from him slightly and looked down at the ground. "You're not the only one who needs to be more accommodating sometimes, Ross," she admitted with a rueful sigh. She knew she was too stubborn for her own good at times, that she could be every bit as willful as Kimberly and Ross combined. She looked up at him again, meaning every word of her throatily voiced promise.

"It really wouldn't kill me to let you drive me home if the weather's bad, especially if it'll make you feel better. Also, I can let you help me with some of the heavy manual chores." She raised her index finger and laid out the rest of her conditions. "Just so long as you don't let me slip back into my former overly dependent habits. I don't want to suddenly turn into a helpless ninny who needs a man's help just to turn on a water faucet or carry in a sack of groceries.

Ross's laughter was velvet soft. "I promise I won't let you do that—ever." He lifted his hand, as if taking an oath.

Linda smiled back at him, amazed and thrilled they had come to a solution. "Then it's settled?" Linda said, searching his eyes for confirmation, her relief shimmering through her in giant waves.

He nodded affirmatively. "We start over," he said without hesitation.

"Or better yet," Linda amended, "take up where we left off."

Ross's eyes darkened and he kissed her passionately. "Either way, I still love you," he said quietly, drawing her more fully into his arms. He kissed her brow and held her tightly against him. "And I want us to try again."

Joy made Linda giddy. She wreathed her arms about his neck and for long moments just enjoyed the closeness, the tender promise she heard in his voice. "Oh, Ross, do you mean it?" she whispered, thinking this was almost too good to be true.

He held her even tighter. "You bet I mean it. We've got too much going for us to throw it all away." His kiss was slow and soft and deep. "No one's ever made me feel the way you do, Linda. No one."

She closed her eyes and nestled deeper into his embrace. She hugged him tighter. "I love you, too," she said softly, "so much. Oh, Ross, we'll do better this time, you'll see."

"I know we will." He bent and kissed her chin. And then her nose. And then her hand.

Linda laughed, enjoying his newly playful mood. He had certainly surprised her today.

But she couldn't let him take all the blame. "Ross, you were right about there being a certain responsibility that comes with having children. You can't just think about yourself anymore." As Wendy had for a brief while. "You have to put the child first. I know you've already been doing that—"

"A little too much sometimes," he interjected dryly.

"—but I can do that, too," she returned passionately. And she also wanted to spend time with Ross and with Kimberly. Lots and lots of quality time.

Hearing her plans, Ross smiled and kissed her again. "Sounds good to me."

"It had better," Linda murmured softly in response, holding him close, "because this is one set of commitments that comes with a lifetime guarantee!"

CHRISTMAS IS FOR KIDS

Spend this holiday season with nine very special children. Children whose wishes come true at the magical time of Christmas.

Read American Romance's CHRISTMAS IS FOR KIDS—heartwarming holiday stories in which children bring together four couples who fall in love. Meet:

Frank, Dorcas, Kathy, Candy and Nicky—They become friends at St. Christopher's orphanage, but they really want to be adopted and become part of a real family, in #321 *A Carol Christmas* by Muriel Jensen.

Patty—She's a ten-year-old certified genius, but she wants what every little girl wishes for: a daddy of her own, in #322 *Mrs. Scrooge* by Barbara Bretton.

Amy and Flash—Their mom is about to deliver their newest sibling any day, but Christmas just isn't the same now—not without their dad. More than anything they want their family reunited for Christmas, in #323 *Dear Santa* by Margaret St. George.

Spencer—Living with his dad and grandpa in an all-male household has its advantages, but Spence wants Santa to bring him a mommy to love, in #324 *The Best Gift of All* by Andrea Davidson.

These children will win your hearts as they entice—and matchmake—the adults into a true romance. This holiday, invite them—and the four couples they bring together—into your home.

Look for all four CHRISTMAS IS FOR KIDS books coming in December from Harlequin American Romance. And happy holidays!

XMAS-KIDS-1

HARLEQUIN
American Romance

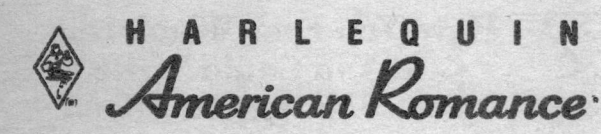

COMING NEXT MONTH

#321 A CAROL CHRISTMAS by Muriel Jensen

The children wanted a family to belong to. It was their last Christmas together. Housemother Carol Shaw wanted to make it special for Frank, Docras, Kathy and Candy—children who'd never had a family and faced an uncertain future in foster homes. Help arrived when baseball pro Mike Rafferty came to St. Christopher's. Mike brought excitement into all their lives. And then the snow came, bringing with it Carol's dearest wish for her charges. Mike, Carol and the children were going to celebrate the holiday as a family, with joy and love.

#322 MRS. SCROOGE by Barbara Bretton

All Patty wanted was a father of her own. Normally, chemistry didn't present a challenge to ten-year-old genius Patty. But man-woman chemistry was a different thing, and it had Patty stumped. Patty thought she only had to find the perfect father, introduce him to Mom and the rest would take care of itself. But Mom and Murphy O'Rourke weren't showing any signs of chemistry. Maybe chemistry was like magic—somehow, suddenly, it just happened. So maybe Patty didn't have to worry, for the most magical things happened at Christmas.

#323 DEAR SANTA by Margaret St. George

Flash and Amy wanted to be a family again. Their dad's job kept him in Los Angeles. Amy and Flash lived with their mother in Aspen Springs, which was supposed to be a great place for kids. But Amy and Flash knew where they all belonged—together. It wasn't easy convincing parents too stubborn to admit they were in love. So Amy got a pencil and paper, and wrote a letter to Santa....

#324 THE BEST GIFT OF ALL by Andrea Davidson

All Spence wanted was a mother to love. Spence Carruthers had a room full of toys, a live-in grandfather who knew all about fishing and a father who'd forgotten how to count his blessings. Mark Carruthers had run so hard and so long from childhood poverty that he'd lost sight of what he had here and now. Leah helped Mark remember. Leah brought the spirit of Christmas into the Carruthers' home. To Spence it was warm and comforting—like a mother's love.

Have You Ever Wondered If You Could Write A Harlequin Novel?

Here's great news—Harlequin is offering a series of cassette tapes to help you do just that. Written by Harlequin editors, these tapes give practical advice on how to make your characters—and your story—come alive. There's a tape for each contemporary romance series Harlequin publishes.

Mail order only

All sales final

TO: **Harlequin Reader Service**
Audiocassette Tape Offer
P.O. Box 1396
Buffalo, NY 14269-1396

I enclose a check/money order payable to HARLEQUIN READER SERVICE® for $9.70 ($8.95 plus 75¢ postage and handling) for EACH tape ordered for the total sum of $_____*
Please send:

☐ Romance and Presents   ☐ Intrigue
☐ American Romance   ☐ Temptation
☐ Superromance   ☐ All five tapes ($38.80 total)

Signature_____
                                                (please print clearly)
Name:_____
Address:_____
State:_____ Zip:_____

*Iowa and New York residents add appropriate sales tax.

AUDIO-H

Summer of '89 Subscribers-only Sweepstakes

INDULGE A LITTLE—WIN A LOT!

This month's prize:

A CARIBBEAN CRUISE
Vacation for Two!

Are you the Reader Service subscriber who is going to win a *free* Caribbean cruise vacation? The facing page contains two entry forms, as does each of the other books you received in this shipment. Complete and return *all* entry forms—the more you send in, the better your chances of winning!

Then keep your fingers crossed, because you'll find out by November 7, 1989 if you're this month's winner! And if you are, here's what you'll get:

- **Round-trip airfare for two to San Juan, where you'll board a Chandris Fantasy Cruise for a one-week Caribbean adventure!**
- **Ports of call typically include St. Thomas, Guadeloupe, Barbados, St. Lucia, Antigua, and St. Maarten.**
- **Lavish meals are served, and there's plenty to do on board, including swimming, sauna, dancing, casino gambling, skeet shooting, movies and nightclub entertainment— all included!**
- **A daily cash allowance (as determined by the enclosed "Wallet" scratch-off card)!**

Remember, this is a random drawing *not* open to the general public. The more Official Entry Forms you send in, the better your chances of winning!

> Coming next month:
> Win a 3-island HAWAIIAN vacation for 2!
> No purchase necessary. See rules for details.

DLIBC-2

SHE WAS THE YOUNGEST CHILD

Linda Harrigan—always the pampered, charming youngest, even as she approached her mid-thirties—finally wanted to break out on her own, to take some risks. Her state-of-the-art day-care center seemed the answer to her prayers.

Banker Ross Hollister was willing to help. He lent capital as a silent partner and himself as a warm, receptive friend.

The charmer was charmed—until the first crisis, when Ross's protective tendencies turned overprotective and he threatened the very dreams she most cherished.

ISBN 0-373-16318-5